# Feeling bold, Mano traced the neckline of Paige's gown with his finger, finding the V plunged deep.

His fingertip lingered at the apex for a moment as Paige let out a ragged breath. He expected her to pull away or tell him to stop, but she didn't. She leaned closer to him. The scent of her mingled with the plumeria and orchids that perfumed the breezes. He was intoxicated by it and drawn to her in a way he simply didn't understand.

Gently cupping her face in his hands, he lowered his lips to hers. Her response to him was cautious, but curious. After a moment, the caution gave way to enthusiasm. She wrapped her arms around his neck and arched her body against him. Mano felt his every muscle tighten as her lithe body pressed into his own.

He let his tongue explore her mouth as his hands explored her body. As his hand strayed near her belly, she went stiff as stone in his arms. "Paige?"

He felt her pull away and the next thing he knew, her loud and unsteady clomp of heels against the hardwood floors grew softer and softer until the front door of his suite slammed shut.

He'd had a lot of reactions to his kisses in his life, but he'd never had a woman turn tail and run.

\* \* \*

*The Pregnancy Proposition* is part of the Hawaiian Nights series— Paradise changes everything!

Dear Reader,

Last year, I took a trip to Hawaii and I knew immediately that I wanted to set a duet of books there. My trip to the USS *Arizona* inspired the starting point for this book and gave me the reason for Paige to come to Hawaii for the first time. I'd also been toying with the idea of doing a blind hero and I decided that this was my chance.

So much of Hawaii is visual, and I looked forward to experiencing the island through the other four senses the way Mano does. In the book, he also gets to experience it all through the eyes of Paige as she sees it for the first time. She was another character I was excited to write—she's not pretty, she's not curvy—at best, she's plain and awkward. She can't understand why a man like Mano would want anything to do with her. That's when the fun starts.

If you enjoy Mano and Paige's story, tell me by visiting my website at www.andrealaurence.com, like my fan page on Facebook or follow me on Twitter.

Enjoy,

*Andrea*

# ANDREA LAURENCE

---

## THE PREGNANCY PROPOSITION

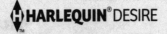HARLEQUIN®DESIRE

Recycling programs
for this product may
not exist in your area.

ISBN-13: 978-0-373-73488-7

The Pregnancy Proposition

Copyright © 2016 by Andrea Laurence

**Printed in U.S.A.**

HARLEQUIN®
www.Harlequin.com

**Andrea Laurence** is an award-winning author of contemporary romances filled with seduction and sass. She has been a lover of reading and writing stories since she was young and is thrilled to share her special blend of sensuality and dry, sarcastic humor with readers. A dedicated West Coast girl transplanted into the Deep South, she's working on her own happily-ever-after with her boyfriend and their collection of animals.

### Books by Andrea Laurence

### Harlequin Desire

#### *Brides and Belles*

*Snowed In with Her Ex*
*Thirty Days to Win His Wife*
*One Week with the Best Man*
*A White Wedding Christmas*

#### *Secrets of Eden*

*Undeniable Demands*
*A Beauty Uncovered*
*Heir to Scandal*
*Her Secret Husband*

#### *Millionaires of Manhattan*

*What Lies Beneath*
*More Than He Expected*
*His Lover's Little Secret*
*The CEO's Unexpected Child*

#### *Hawaiian Nights*

*The Pregnancy Proposition*

Visit her Author Profile page at Harlequin.com, or andrealaurence.com, for more titles.

To my boss Lawanda and my coworker LT—

You were right, Hawaii was worth the long flight.
Thanks for covering for me whenever
my writing takes me around the world and
being so supportive of my writing alter ego.

# One

"Well, Papa, you finally made it back to Hawaii."

Paige Edwards gripped her grandfather's urn as she followed the driver to the town car waiting outside the Honolulu airport. He loaded her bags and opened the door for her to climb into the backseat.

As they drove through the busy, winding streets toward her hotel on Waikiki beach, she couldn't dismiss the surreal feeling that had hovered over her for the last few weeks. It started with the call from her mother to tell her that her grandfather had finally passed on. For the last year, he'd battled with congestive heart failure. As a nurse, Paige had felt the need to spend time with him and ensure he was receiving the best possible care.

It wasn't really necessary. Her grandfather was ridiculously wealthy and could afford the best doctors and treatments in Southern California. But she cared, and so she'd spent a lot of time there. Toward the end, it was easier than facing how big of a mess her life had become.

And once her grandfather died, she was able to distract herself with the plans for his memorial service and listening to her parents fret about how the estate would be divided.

Paige honestly didn't care about that. Papa's money was always there in the background, but it wasn't something she felt the need to clamor for. She'd actually encouraged her grandfather to donate his money to a cause that was important to him. That would cut down on the sharks circling around his estate.

What she hadn't been prepared for, however, was that her grandfather had bigger plans for her than she had ever expected. Those plans had forced her to pack her bags and get on a plane to Hawaii with his ashes.

Looking out the window, she could understand why her grandfather would want to have his ashes left in Hawaii. It was beautiful. As they got closer to the hotel, she could spy glimpses of golden sand and turquoise waters against the cloudless blue sky. Palm trees swayed in the breeze and people in various states of beach dress crowded the sidewalks and outdoor eateries.

The car finally slowed to turn into a resort named the Mau Loa. Paige hadn't really paid a lot of attention to the details of the itinerary her grandfather's executor had put together. This wasn't supposed to be about a vacation for her, so she didn't care where she stayed.

When they stopped outside and the bellhop opened the car door, she realized that her grandfather had had very different ideas about this trip.

This wasn't a Holiday Inn five blocks from the beach. It was on the beach itself. The bellman was in a nice uniform with pristine white gloves. The entryway was open to the breezes, allowing a view through the lobby to the ocean beyond it.

The bellman escorted her to the VIP check-in station. She handed over the paperwork the executor gave her, and the woman at the counter's eyes widened for a moment before a large smile crossed her face.

"Aloha, Miss Edwards. Welcome to the Mau Loa." She came out from behind the desk to drape a lei of magenta orchids around her neck. They smelled like heaven.

The woman then turned to the bellhop with her bags. "Please take Miss Edwards's things to the Aolani Suite and then let Mr. Bishop know we have a new VIP guest checking in."

Paige's eyebrows rose. A suite? VIP? Papa really had gone all out, although it wasn't necessary. As a nurse at a veteran's hospital, she wasn't used to being pampered. She spent most of her time chasing away nighttime demons from traumatized ex-soldiers and trying to convince them that losing their leg wasn't the end of the world. The suicide rate was far too high amongst the servicemen and women who returned home. Pampering herself seemed a little ridiculous after coming home from that day after day.

She glanced around as the woman completed her check-in. Beyond the lobby, a trio of men were playing instruments by a lagoon-like pool with a waterfall. An employee was lighting torches around the area as the sun started to go down. The sound of the waves mingled with the melody of the traditional Hawaiian music, and Paige could almost feel her blood pressure lowering.

She had only made it ten feet into the hotel and she already knew she adored Hawaii.

"Here is your key card, Miss Edwards. Your suite is ready for you now. Just follow the pathway through the garden to the Sunset Tower. There will be live music until ten by the pool. Enjoy your stay."

"Thank you." Paige took the key and started down the stone path toward her hotel room.

The resort was large, with multiple towers surrounding a common courtyard. *Courtyard* didn't really do it justice, actually. There was the massive pool with a waterfall and a pair of slides, multiple restaurants and tropical plants at every turn. It was like a lush garden in the middle of the rainforest.

The Sunset Tower was the closest to the beach. She looked at her key as she entered the elevator. Her suite was room 2001. Paige tried not to frown as she pushed the button and the elevator spirited her up twenty stories to the top floor. As the doors opened, she expected a long hallway, but instead found herself in a small vestibule. To her left was a door marked Private. To the right was the door to room 2001 with a plaque that noted it was called the Aolani Suite. Where were the rest of the rooms on this floor?

She was about to slip her card into the lock when the door opened and the bellman came out. He held the door open for her. "Your bags are in the master bedroom suite. Enjoy your stay at the Mau Loa."

He got back on the elevator and disappeared, leaving her standing in the doorway at a complete loss. She crept into the room and let the door swing shut behind her.

This couldn't be right. This was…the penthouse suite.

It was bigger than her apartment and made almost entirely of windows. It had a living room with plush leather couches and a big-screen television, a dining room table that seated eight and a kitchen with state-of-the-art appliances. The neutral color palette, pale wood floors, white furniture and shiny modern metallic accents created a sleek, clean design that was very soothing. One side of the room overlooked downtown Honolulu, the other overlooked Waikiki.

Paige was immediately drawn to the balcony over the ocean. She shifted her grandfather's urn in her arms to slide the glass panel door open and step outside. The breeze immediately caught her long, straight brown hair, blowing it around her face. She brushed it aside and approached the railing to take in the view.

It was stunning. The colors all around her were jewel-like. Diamond Head crater stood like a sentinel guarding the beach on her far left. The crescent of pale sand edged the water, which was dotted with surfers. A pod of dolphins leapt through the waves, spiraling through the air and splashing back into the sea. It was unreal.

"Papa, what have you done?" she asked. But inside, she knew what this was about.

Yes, her grandfather wanted his ashes to be in Honolulu. He had been one of the few remaining survivors of the Pearl Harbor attack that sunk his ship, the USS *Arizona*. As such, he had the option of returning to the ship to be interred. The ceremony was a week away.

Until then, however, this trip was all about her. There was no other reason that his service would require her to fly first class or stay in the penthouse suite of a five-star hotel. He had done this for her. And boy, was she grateful. Paige's life had taken an unexpected turn recently, and a week in Hawaii was exactly what she needed to figure out what the hell she was going to do.

With a sigh, she stepped back into the suite and set her grandfather's urn on a nearby table. Beside it was a large wicker basket overflowing with fresh fruits, cookies, macadamia nut candies and other local delicacies. Tucked inside was an envelope that said "Miss Edwards" on the outside. She opened it and read the card on the fancy, embossed Mau Loa stationary.

*"Welcome to the Mau Loa. We hope your stay is a magical one. Aloha."*

"Aloha," she replied to the empty room, putting the card back on the table.

Looking at her watch, she realized it was a good time for dinner. She was fresh off a few weeks on the night shift at the hospital. Combining that with a long flight and time change, she was exhausted. But she had to eat. If she hurried, she might be able to watch the sunset. Paige rushed to her bedroom and opened her luggage. She traded her jeans and sneakers for a sundress and a pair of bejeweled sandals. That was all she needed.

She grabbed her purse and her room key and set out to enjoy her first night on Oahu while she could keep her eyes open.

Pulling the door closed, she turned toward the elevator and slammed into a solid wall of muscle. As she stumbled back, a man's hand sought out her elbow to steady her. The man was several inches over six feet, making Paige seem petite at five-foot-ten. He wasn't just tall; he was large, with broad shoulders and biceps the size of her calves beneath his tailored suit. He had on a pair of classic black Ray-Ban sunglasses and a black earpiece that curved behind his ear and blended with the dark brown waves of his collar-length hair.

What she could see of the man's face was unbelievably handsome, and—she quickly noted—completely out of her league. But that didn't keep her body from clenching in response to such a potent specimen of man nearby. Her surprised intake of breath drew in his scent, a heady mix of musk and male that sent an unexpected shiver of need down her spine even as she recovered from their collision.

"I'm so sorry!" she exclaimed as she gathered herself. "I was in such a hurry I didn't see you there." The fact that she'd missed such a mountain of a man right in front of her was a testament to how scattered her thoughts were lately.

The man smiled, flashing bright white teeth against the warm tan of his Polynesian skin. The slight hint of a dimple in his cheek made her knees soften. "That's okay. I didn't see you, either."

Paige noticed the man didn't look directly at her

as he spoke. Glancing down, she spotted the large chocolate brown Labrador retriever on his other side. In a service dog harness.

*Good job, Paige.* She'd just plowed into a handsome, incredibly sexy blind man.

"Ohmigosh," the woman said with increased angst in her voice. Apparently, she had gotten his joke but hadn't found it funny. Few people found blind jokes amusing, but he'd developed a dark sense of humor over the last ten years where his disability was concerned.

"Are you okay?" she continued.

Mano had to laugh. He might be blind, but he was hardly fragile. The woman could've plowed into him at a full run and he would've hardly felt it. "I'm fine. Are you all right?"

"Yes. Just embarrassed."

Mano could almost envision the blush that rose to the young woman's cheeks. He didn't imagine that many of the women he met on a day-to-day basis blushed much. This one seemed different from the usual guests of the Aolani Suite, though—nervous and easily flustered. The kind of money it took to afford that room usually came with a certain hardness that he didn't detect from her.

"Don't be embarrassed," he soothed. "Feel free to run into me whenever you like. I'm Mano Bishop, the owner of the hotel. I was just on my way to welcome the newest guest of the Aolani Suite. That means you must be Miss Edwards." He switched Hōkū's lead to his left hand and held out his right to her.

"Yes," she said, taking the hand he offered and shaking it. "Paige, please."

The touch of her small hand in his sent a bolt of awareness down his spine, forcing him to shift on his feet. The unexpected thrill made Mano take a more thorough notice of his new guest. She didn't just sound unlike his usual penthouse guest, she felt different, too. Her skin wasn't as soft as he expected a young woman's to be. There was a roughness to it as though she worked with her hands. It made him wonder if she was an artist of some kind. She certainly wasn't a pampered princess. "How did you find the suite, Paige? I hope it met your expectations."

"It's amazing. I mean, it's more beautiful than I ever expected it to be. And the view is incredible. Of course you know what...*er*...oh dear."

"Actually, I do," he interjected quickly, saving her from her awkward statement. "I didn't lose my sight until I was seventeen. I may not be able to see the view any longer, but I remember it well."

The elevator chimed and the doors opened. He heard Paige's sigh of relief and tried to hide his smile.

"Please—" he gestured "—go ahead." He listened for the shuffling of her movement as she got on the elevator, then Hōkū pulled at his harness and led Mano into the elevator behind her. He ran his hands over the control panel, finding the lobby button marked with the braille symbol. Then he turned to face the door and reached for the railing to steady himself.

"What is your service dog's name?" Paige asked as they descended.

"This is Hōkū," he said. The brown lab had been at his side for seven years, and he'd become almost a part of Mano. "You may pet him if you like."

"Are you sure? I know you're not supposed to do that when they're working."

Smart. Most people didn't know that. "Unfortunately, I am always working, so Hōkū is always working. Give him a pet, he'll love you forever."

"Hello, Hōkū," Paige said in the high voice people reserved for babies and animals. "Are you a good boy?"

She was rewarded with Hōkū's heavy, happy panting. She was probably scratching his ears. He was a sucker for a good ear scratching.

"What does *Hōkū* mean?"

Mano enjoyed the melodic quality of Paige's voice, especially as she used some of his native Hawaiian language. It wasn't too deep or too high, but he could hear the smile when she spoke. "It means 'star' in Hawaiian. Before navigation systems and maps, sailors used to guide their ships by the stars, and since I use him to guide me, I thought that was an appropriate choice."

"That's perfect."

A cloud of her scent rose up as she stood. Paige had a unique fragrance, and yet it was somehow very familiar to him. Many women, especially those from the Aolani suite, nearly bathed in expensive perfumes or scented lotions. Most people wouldn't even notice it, but Mano was overpowered by smells, good and bad. Paige's scent was subtle but appealing, like a hint of baby powder and a touch of…hand sanitizer. That was a different combination.

The elevator chimed and the system announced that they were on the lobby level. He'd had the elevators updated several years back to include that feature for himself and any other visually impaired guests. The doors opened and he held out his hand for Paige to exit ahead of him. He expected her to rush out the door toward her destination. Most people were a little uncomfortable around him. She obviously was, but it didn't repel her. Her scent lingered at his side as he exited.

"Are you eating dinner at the hotel tonight?" he asked.

"That's where I was headed. I'm not sure where I'm going yet."

"If you want your first meal to be an authentic

one, I would recommend Lani. That is our traditional Polynesian restaurant, so you'll get a great taste of what Honolulu has to offer in its culinary basket. There's also a beautiful outdoor seating area. If you hurry, I believe you can still catch the sunset. It's not to be missed. Just tell the hostess that I sent you and she'll make sure you get the best seat available."

"Thank you. I'll do that. I hope we'll see each other...*er*...run into each other again soon."

Mano smiled as she stumbled over her words again. "Enjoy your evening, Paige. *A hui hou kakou*."

"What does that mean?"

"Until we meet again," he said.

"Oh. Thank you for your help. Good night."

Mano waved casually and then listened as the slap of her sandals faded in the direction of the beach and hotel restaurants. Once she was gone, he turned toward the registration desks and let Hōkū lead him through the guests. Hōkū stopped just short of the counter where they went through the swinging door to enter the area behind the registration desk. The concierge station was just to his right.

"*Aloha ahiahi*, Mr. Bishop."

"Good evening, Neil. How are things going tonight?"

"Fine. You've just missed the check-in rush from all the stateside flights arriving."

Good. He did well to move about the hotel, but

he tried to avoid the busiest times when he was most likely to run into an issue with people dragging roller bags or children running around.

Since it wasn't busy at the moment, he also wondered if he could take advantage of his concierge's eyes. He was curious about his new guest, Paige. "Did you happen to see the young woman that got off the elevator with me?"

"Briefly, sir. I didn't get a good look at her."

It amazed Mano sometimes how those with sight spent most of their time not taking full advantage of it. "What of her did you see?"

"Just a basic impression because I noticed her speaking with you. She was tall for a woman; with long, straight brown hair. Pale. Very thin. I didn't really see her face since she was turned toward you."

Mano nodded. That could've described a thousand women at the hotel, easily. It was a start, though. "Okay, thank you. Let me know if you have any issues. I'll be in my office."

"Yes, sir."

Mano and Hōkū continued down a hallway and through the area where hotel management worked to keep things flowing smoothly. They went down another hallway and turned to enter his office. He flipped on the light and made his way to his desk. Neither he nor Hōkū needed the light, but he'd discovered that his employees found it strange that he

would sit in a dark office and would think he didn't
want to be disturbed.

Mano settled into his chair and Hōkū curled up
to sleep at his feet. His dog always laid his head on
his shoe, so Mano knew he was there. He leaned
down to pat the dog on the head, hit a few keys on
the keyboard to wake up his computer and slipped
the headset he used to control it over his free ear.
It allowed his system to read emails and files to
him, and he could control it with voice commands.
He wished he could tell his high school keyboard-
ing teacher that no, he wouldn't need that skill in
the future.

As he checked his email, his attention was drawn
to his other earpiece that was connected to the hotel
security system. Mano knew everything that happened at his hotel even if he couldn't see it occur. It
had been a quiet day with a lot of idle chatter. That
would change as the sun went down. The weekends
got a little wilder at the resort with nightly luaus,
fireworks shows and plenty of mai tais to go around.

At the moment, two members of his team were
trying to determine if a gentleman at the outdoor
bar needed to be cut off. He was getting loud. Mano
didn't worry about those kinds of issues. His staff
could handle them easily.

A soft tap sounded at his door. Mano looked up
expectantly toward the sound. "Yes?"

"Good evening, Mr. Bishop."

Mano recognized the voice as his head of operations, Chuck. They had grown up together and had been friends in school since second grade. "Evening, Chuck. Anything of note happen while I went upstairs?"

"No, sir."

"Good. Listen, did you happen to be around when our Aolani VIP checked in this afternoon?"

"I was not, but Wendy was at the desk around that time. I can check with her if you need something."

Mano shook his head. He felt a little silly even asking, but it wasn't as though he could find out otherwise. "Don't trouble her, no. But if you happen to see Miss Edwards, let me know what you think. She seemed…different. She piqued my curiosity."

"Hmm…" Chuck said in a tone that Mano didn't like. "If she's caught your interest, I want to get an eyeful for myself. It's been a long time since you allowed yourself a little companionship. Could she be your latest lucky selection?"

Mano sighed. Chuck would likely torture him mercilessly now. He was a lot like his older brother, Kal, in that way. It was his own fault for telling his friend about his unusual dating habits, but it was the only thing that kept people from trying to fix him up all the time. "I don't know about that. I just wanted your opinion before I ask her to dinner tomorrow evening."

"So you *are* asking her out to dinner?" Chuck asked.

"Not on a date," Mano corrected. "I was going to ask her to join me at the owner's table." It was a tradition his grandfather started at the hotel, and he had carried it on when he took over. It was just the first time it involved a young woman traveling on her own. "I was curious about her being here by herself."

Chuck was right to a point, although Mano wouldn't tell him so. He was interested in Paige. He didn't like dating guests at the hotel, but considering he almost never left the property, it was that or celibacy. From time to time, if he found a woman who interested him, he'd propose that she spend a week with him. No strings, no emotions, just a few days of fantasy before she returned home to her regular life. That's all he was willing to offer a woman. At least since Jenna.

His personal experiences had taught him that a short-term fantasy was the best thing he had to offer. His disability always seemed like the third wheel of every relationship. He may have adjusted to being blind, but he hated to ask someone else to deal with it long-term. He did his best not to be a burden on his family, but it would be harder to shield a woman in his life from it. He didn't want to be a burden on the woman he loved.

"I'll look into it, sir."

Chuck disappeared, leaving Mano to return to his work. He started to give a voice command, but he stopped. He wasn't really interested in reading any more emails tonight. Mano was far more intrigued by the idea of going down to Lani and finding out more about this mysterious Paige. He wanted to sit and listen to her speak a while longer. He wanted to draw in more of her scent and find out exactly what bizarre combination she was wearing. He wanted to know why her hands were so rough and why she was staying all alone in such a huge suite in such a romantic location.

He considered it for a moment, then dismissed the idea as foolish. It was her first night in Hawaii. Certainly she had better things to do with her evening than to tell her life story to the blind, lonely owner of the hotel. Yes, she'd intrigued him, and yes, her mere touch had lit all the nerve endings in his body, but she didn't necessarily have the same reaction to him. He was handsome enough, or at least he was the last time he'd seen his own reflection. But there was no overlooking his disability.

Pushing the thought and sensation of her touch aside, he barked out another command to his computer and continued to work.

But perhaps he'd get his answers tomorrow night.

# Two

Holy jet lag, Batman.

Paige found herself wide awake the next morning before the sunrise. It was only a three-hour time difference from San Diego, but she hadn't been able to sleep that night. A long stint on nights before her vacation had her clock all turned around. But with a return to sleep eluding her, she decided to stop fighting it. She got dressed and headed downstairs with her camera in the hopes that she could catch some nice pictures of the sunrise.

The hotel was quiet and mostly dark. The occasional employee walked by as they readied the hotel for morning, but she was the only guest in sight.

Even the coffee shop was still closed. It was just as well, she supposed. Coffee was on the no-no list her doctor had given her. She was limited in how much caffeine she could have, and she'd rather get it from chocolate. At least when she wasn't awake at 5:00 a.m. Later today, she might feel differently.

Recently, Paige wished she could drink something a little stronger than coffee. Her grandfather's death was just the latest news to upend her world. Before that, she'd gotten wrapped up in an unexpectedly passionate relationship with a man named Wyatt. He was a landscaper working for her grandfather, and they'd met while she'd been there taking care of Papa. She'd never expected such a handsome man to pay any attention to a woman like her. He had shaggy blond hair, a deep tan and strong hands. His dark blue eyes focusing on her was a welcome change after years of being looked over in favor of her pretty and popular older sister, Piper.

Paige knew she wasn't what most men wanted. It wasn't so much a matter of self-esteem as it was fact. She was thin without any hips or breasts to speak of. Her face was oddly angular, and her skin was ghostly pale despite living in sunny San Diego. After spending all of her hours working at the VA hospital and taking no time for herself, Wyatt's attentions were like a breath of fresh air. At least until the dream turned into a nightmare. Two months into their relationship, Wyatt dumped Paige for Piper. And a month after that, Paige found out she was pregnant with his child.

She was a nurse. She knew better than to skip protection in the rush of desire. And yet it had happened, anyway. Paige felt like such a fool. Wyatt had seemed so sincere in his attraction to her. All her guards went down and the next thing she knew, she was heartbroken with a bad case of morning sickness. She hadn't spoken to her sister since Wyatt left her.

Before she could figure out what to do about the mess she was in, her grandfather had died and shifted her focus. She had about six months to deal with the impending arrival of the baby. Her grandfather's death and final wishes were a more immediate issue.

Paige couldn't ignore it forever, though. Like it or not, she needed to start telling people about her pregnancy, including Wyatt and her sister. She needed to get a bigger apartment so she could decorate a nursery. She needed to tell her boss about her upcoming maternity leave. So far, she'd kept it all a secret to herself. Only her doctor knew.

It was a lot to think about, but it was easy to forget all that as she kicked off her sandals and stepped onto the sand. Paige hadn't told her grandfather about what happened with Wyatt, and yet he seemed to know she was unhappy. His final gift to her couldn't have had better timing.

With her shoes in one hand and her camera in the other, she ventured out to the shoreline. The sky was starting to lighten, making everything a dull gray before the brilliance of sunrise. A few dedicated joggers ran past her on the footpath that followed the Waikiki shore. A couple surfers were tugging on their wetsuits and preparing to paddle out. Day was arriving.

Approaching the ocean, she stopped as the cool water washed up over her bare feet. It was then that the magic happened. The rising sun started illuminating the sky in beautiful pastel shades of blue, pink and purple. The palm trees and boats in the harbor were black silhouettes against the horizon.

Paige took a few photos, then watched as the shape of Diamond Head crater grew more pronounced and the sun rose above it. Daylight had finally arrived in earnest. The whole island seemed to wake up then.

As Paige turned back to the hotel, she noticed employees setting up chairs and putting out towels around the pool. A larger crowd was walking up and down the jogging path now, and some were sitting on benches along the beach with their cups of coffee.

She suddenly had a burning need for a skinny

mocha latte. She'd have to soothe the urge with a vanilla steamer to get that calcium in.

Back on the sidewalk, Paige rinsed the sand off her feet at the provided foot wash and slipped back into her sandals. She followed the winding path through the dense, dark foliage that would lead back to her room. At some point, she took the wrong fork in the sidewalk and ended up in an unfamiliar area of the resort. There was a large stretch of green lawn, and beyond it was the sandy lagoon where guests could paddleboard or practice snorkeling.

She also found the owner of the hotel and his dog out there. Paige almost didn't recognize Mano in his jeans and a fitted T-shirt. He seemed like the kind of man who wore a suit to sleep in. Then again... why would he go to all that trouble just to take his dog downstairs for an early morning potty break?

She certainly didn't mind seeing him again. She'd relived their encounter all evening. Just the sight of him again made her cheeks burn with embarrassment and her body tingle with the memory of his innocent touch. She'd reacted to him instantly in a way that was extremely inappropriate for someone she'd just met. Paige didn't know if it was the pregnancy hormones getting the best of her or the superromantic environment, but she'd lain in bed all night, aching and unfulfilled with thoughts of the hotel owner on her mind.

His muscles were even more defined than in the

suit he'd worn yesterday. He might be blind, but he clearly knew how to find his way to the hotel gym. His brown, nearly black hair was mussed but swept back from his face as though he'd combed through it quickly with his fingers. From a distance, she could make out some kind of tribal tattoo on his left forearm. Just the thought of tracing her fingers over the design made her stomach clench with a renewed need.

Paige immediately tried to suppress the feeling as she had the night before. The last time she'd let herself fall prey to her desires she ended up pregnant and alone. She couldn't get pregnant this time, but that didn't mean she couldn't do something else stupid.

Before she could turn and try to find her way back to her room, she noticed that Hōkū saw her standing there. His cheesy Labrador grin was wide and his tail wagged so frantically his whole bottom wiggled from the force of it. Paige realized that Mano recognized the change in the dog and knew she needed to make her presence known.

"Good morning, Paige," he said before she could greet him.

She walked the last few feet across the lawn to where Mano and Hōkū were standing. "Good morning," she said, patting the dog on the head. "How did you know I was out here?"

"You're wearing the same sandals you had on yesterday. They make a very distinctive clip-clop sound when you walk. I could also smell you coming."

Paige frowned and tried to sniff discreetly at her armpits. She hadn't taken a shower yet that morning, but it couldn't be that bad. Could it? Here she was fantasizing about the sexy hotelier while he was noting how bad she smelled. She was marching straight upstairs and scrubbing every inch of her body with the provided coconut soaps.

"Relax," Mano added when she didn't respond. "It's not a bad scent, just a distinctive one."

She wasn't sure how he knew she was silently panicking, but she was glad she wasn't recognizable by her trademark funk. "Thank goodness," she said with a sigh.

Mano smiled, revealing his blinding white teeth against his rich, tanned skin. He truly was an amazingly handsome man. Last night, she'd wondered if perhaps she'd embellished him in her mind. No man could really be that attractive. But now that she looked up at him again, she realized it was true. Paige had thought Wyatt was good looking, but he couldn't hold a candle to Mano. Not even the T-shirt and slightly askew morning hair could dampen his masculine appeal.

He was a strange juxtaposition of traits that seemed incompatible in her mind. He had heavy, sharp eyebrows over his sunglasses, one with a scar that sliced through it. It made him look more like he should be an ancient warrior or in some badass motorcycle gang instead of the suit-clad owner of an exclusive hotel. Upon closer inspection, she could see that his forearm tattoo was of some kind of black triangle design. That sealed his bad-boy appeal in her mind. It also made her wonder what else his professional suit and polite demeanor were hiding.

Paige had always had a thing for the bad boys. It wasn't practical, or really even smart, but most of the time they didn't give her a second glance, so she couldn't get herself in too much trouble. Wyatt had been the first bad boy to look back at her. Giving in to that attraction had landed her on the path to single parenthood. Even knowing that didn't make her take the step back from Mano that she knew she should.

He never looked at her directly, but she could feel his attention completely fixated in her direction as though he knew she was admiring him. "Do you have plans this evening, Paige?"

Paige frowned. She really didn't have plans for the week. The only thing on the books was the memorial service on Friday. "I don't have plans at all. I figured I would talk to the concierge about booking a few things this week, but right now, I'm winging the whole vacation."

"Are you the kind that normally wings a vacation?"

"God, no," she admitted. "I'm a super planner, but this was a bit of a last minute adventure for me.

I read some of a travel guide on the flight over, but that's about it."

"A last minute trip to Hawaii to stay in the penthouse suite, eh? There are worse things, I suppose."

Well, she supposed that some people lived a life with random tropical vacations, but Paige wasn't one of them. "I'm not complaining, that's for sure. I do feel a little like I'm flapping in the trade winds, however. I'll feel better once I have a plan."

"Well, start your plans with having dinner with me tonight," he said.

Paige narrowed her gaze at him, wondering if perhaps she'd heard him wrong. It was one thing for her to fantasize about him, but why would a Polynesian god like him want to have dinner with her? Was he just being polite because he knew she was here alone? "*You* want to have dinner with *me*?"

Mano chuckled and shoved his free hand into the pocket of his jeans. "Why is that such a ridiculous proposition? You eat, don't you?"

"Well, yes, of course I eat. It's just—"

"And you don't have plans, do you?" he interrupted.

"No plans," she confirmed reluctantly. She wasn't sure why the idea of having dinner with him unnerved her so much. She should be relieved. This was one meal she could have with a man where she wouldn't have to worry about him watching her critically across the table the whole time.

She could just imagine her family's response if she told them she was having dinner with a blind man— "He'd be perfect for you!"

Perhaps that was the key to his interest. He didn't know what she looked like. Her sister, Piper, had once suggested she try dating one of her blind patients. The helpful idea in Piper's mind had only sounded cruel in her own head. Maybe her sister was on to something, though.

"Excellent. I'd love for you to join me tonight at the owner's table of The Pearl. It's our seafood restaurant and was rated as one of the best on the island the last five years running. You'll love it."

The owner's table? That made more sense to Paige than the idea of a date or something, although she had to admit she felt a pang of disappointment that went straight to her core. This was some kind of "schmooze with the rich hotel guests" kind of thing. With her luck, he'd probably try to talk her into buying a time-share or something. Mano would certainly be disappointed to find out she wasn't the usual wealthy penthouse guest. Of course, a nice dinner with him was certainly better than anything else she had planned, which was a big nothing all by herself.

"I can give you some suggestions on how to spend your time here," he added almost as if to sweeten the deal, as though a free meal and looking at his handsome face all night wasn't enough.

"Okay," she said at last. "You've talked me into it."

"I usually don't have to try this hard to get a woman to have dinner with me," Mano said with a wry smile. "I was about to be offended."

Paige felt a blush of embarrassment rise to her cheeks. "I didn't mean anything by it. I just can't fathom why you'd want to spend your evening with me."

For the first time, Mano looked at her, as though he were looking into her eyes. Even with his gaze hidden behind his dark glasses, she felt an unexpected connection snap between them and her body reacted. Her tongue felt thick in her mouth as her lips dried out like a desert. Her heart started racing in her rib cage and she suddenly wished this dinner was more than just politeness and tourist tips.

"Why wouldn't I want to spend time with you?" he asked.

Paige didn't want to list out all her flaws. Normally, she didn't have to tell a man what was wrong with her. They knew all too well just by looking at her. "You're busy. And you don't even know me," she replied.

"Hōkū likes you. He's the best judge of character I know. Anyway, by the end of dinner tonight, we won't be strangers any longer. I'll meet you at six."

Paige stood dumbstruck on the lawn as Mano and Hōkū continued on their morning walk. She wasn't quite sure how any of this had happened, but now she was having dinner with him. A bolt of panic shot through her, sending her on a fast path back to her hotel suite.

What was she going to wear?

"She's traveling alone, sir. Her reservations were made and paid through a travel agency. I tried to Google her and I didn't come up with anything but an obituary for her grandfather, who died a few weeks ago in Southern California. She doesn't even have a Facebook account."

Mano listened to Chuck report back on his penthouse guest as he dressed for dinner. "Is my tie straight?" he asked, turning to him.

"Yes, sir. Don't you think it's odd that there's nothing about her anywhere?"

These days it was a rarity, but that didn't mean there was something wrong with it. "Maybe she's mastered the fine art of living under the radar. It's a highly underrated skill these days. Not everyone feels the need to broadcast their every thought and feeling into cyberspace. I don't."

"I was able to get a little information on her deceased grandfather," Chuck added. "Apparently, he was a former military man that went into real estate development after World War II. He's credited with starting the tract house boom of the 1950s, creating affordable housing for returning soldiers to start families. That, along with the population growth in California at the time, made him a fortune."

That was interesting. His shy flower was an heiress to quite a large chunk of money. She certainly didn't act like one. "So her grandfather invented cookie-cutter suburbia? That's quite an accomplishment." Mano straightened his suit coat. "Anything else?"

"I did ask Wendy about her. She handled her check-in."

That caught Mano's attention. "And?"

"She said Miss Edwards was very willowy, tall and thin. She was pale with an unremarkable face."

That was an odd way to describe her. "Unremarkable? Is that good or bad?"

"I don't know, sir."

Mano sighed. People with eyes simply didn't use them the way they should. If he had his sight back, he would study every detail the way he did now with his hands. He'd talked to multiple staff members, and none of them could tell him what Paige looked like. It was as though she was a ghost that only he could sense. "What time is it?"

"Almost six."

"I'd better get going then." Mano made his way through the suite. He counted his steps, knowing his path through the rooms to the front door like the back of his hand. At the door, he whistled for Hōkū and waited for the sound of clicking toenails across the marble floor to come closer. He put on the dog's service harness and gave him a good scratch behind the ears. "Thanks for the information, Chuck."

"Sure thing. Have a nice dinner," he added with a teasing tone that Mano ignored.

Chuck disappeared into the elevator as Mano rang the doorbell and waited for Paige to answer. It took her a moment, probably because she was wearing heels. He heard the slow, unsteady steps approaching the door. She must not be used to wearing dressy shoes.

The door swung open and he was greeted with the scent of the hotel's coconut soap, a touch of Chanel No. 5 and the underlying hint of hand sanitizer he'd come to associate with Paige. His muscles tightened as he drew her into his lungs, making him more eager than he should've been to spend the evening with one of his hotel guests.

"I'm ready," she said, almost breathless.

He took a step back, then offered his arm to escort her over to the elevator. Mano noticed she leaned a bit more on him than he expected. Definitely the heels. It couldn't possibly be that she wanted to huddle close to a blind man, could it? The tightened muscles throughout his whole body hoped so.

"Does Hōkū get to join us for dinner?" she asked as they made their way to the restaurant.

"Yes. Hōkū goes everywhere. Even before I lost

my eyesight, it was the policy of the hotel to welcome all service animals throughout the site. This close to the military base, we've hosted a lot of former military over the years with PTSD and injuries that require assistance. Everyone here knows Hōkū, anyway. The chef is known to make him his own treat to enjoy under the table while we dine."

"I guess that's not a bad job to have. He's like the hotel mascot."

Mano chuckled. "I suppose he kind of is." The doors to the elevator opened and he led her down the path to The Pearl. The restaurant wasn't original to the hotel, but Mano had added it not long after he took over the resort from his grandparents. The hotel was famous in its own right for being the oldest and most authentic resort on Waikiki, but he'd wanted to add something to put it over the top. It had taken him weeks to interview executive chefs and discuss menu plans to complete his vision, but within a few years, they'd earned a Michelin star. Even people who couldn't stay at the hotel went out of their way for reservations at The Pearl for dinner, especially on Saturday nights.

Hōkū slowed ahead of him and Mano knew they were getting close to the restaurant.

"Good evening, Mr. Bishop," the hostess said as the outer doors swung open and the cool blast of air-conditioning hit them. They stepped inside, waiting to be escorted to their table. "Right this way."

"This restaurant is beautiful," Paige said as they wandered back toward his reserved table. "That fish tank is amazing. I don't think I've ever seen a salt water tank that large outside of an aquarium."

Mano had always enjoyed snorkeling as a teenager. When they opened this restaurant, he wanted the centerpiece of the dining area to be a saltwater tank that showcased the beauty under the surface of the ocean just beyond the hotel. "It's a custom designed tank," he said. "It had to be built inside the restaurant otherwise there was no way to get it through the doors. It has over twenty different species of tropical fish, anemones and sea urchins. There's even a small nurse shark. None of which are on the menu," he said with a smile. "That would be a little creepy."

"Here's your table. Your server will be right with you both. Enjoy."

Mano gestured for Paige to take a seat to the left of the curved booth and he sat to the right. Hōkū found a spot beneath the table and curled up, resting his head on the top of Mano's shoe.

"Do you like seafood?" he asked. "I guess I should've asked that this morning when we made plans."

"I do. I'm trying to avoid the fish that's higher in mercury and anything raw, but I've been known to eat my weight in shrimp when the opportunity arises."

"That means the ahi tuna is out, sadly, but if you like coconut, we have an amazing coconut shrimp here. It's served with a spicy pineapple marmalade."

"That sounds wonderful."

Mano ran his fingers over the custom braille menu to see what tonight's fresh catch was. The specials changed depending on what was available each morning at the Honolulu fish auction. He was pleased to find smoked Hawaiian swordfish poached in duck fat with roasted purple sweet potatoes. That was one of his favorites.

"Everything here sounds delicious," Paige said.

"It is. But save room for dessert or you'll regret it."

The server came a moment later, taking their orders. Paige had taken his recommendation of the coconut shrimp with passion fruit rice pilaf. She turned down his suggestion of a mai tai, though, opting instead for a sparkling water. With that done, they handed away their menus and he was finally able to focus on figuring out his newest guest.

"So, Paige, tell me what it is that brought you to Oahu so unexpectedly, and alone?"

"I suppose that isn't normal, especially considering I'm staying in a suite that could sleep a dozen people. I'm actually here for my grandfather. Next Friday, his ashes are being interred at the USS *Arizona*. He arranged this trip for me to bring him here."

That was not the answer he was expecting at all. He hadn't connected her grandfather's recent passing to the trip. "I'm sorry to hear about your grandfather. Were you close?"

"Yes. I took care of him the last few weeks of his life. It was hard to watch the illness eat away at him, but I could tell he was ready to be done with it all. That's when he let go."

He noticed a sadness in her voice that he didn't like. He wished their conversation hadn't taken such a somber turn, but there was nothing he could do about it now. Few came to Hawaii for a funeral, but Paige was the exception to the rule.

"I knew he always wanted to return here when he died, but I never expected to be the one to do it. I thought for certain my parents would come out here for the service, but his instructions were very clear—I was the one to bring him. All the arrangements were made in advance and no one told me what to expect, so when I arrived it was quite a shock. I certainly didn't need the penthouse or the first class airfare. I guess it was his way of taking care of me since I take care of everyone else all the time."

Over the years, Mano had entertained scores of ridiculously wealthy couples vacationing from around the world, corporate bigwigs doing business and the rich and famous of Hollywood looking for a tropical escape. Chuck had mentioned that

Paige's family had money, so he'd assumed that she was just another guest like the rest.

But the more Paige spoke, the more he began to doubt his assumptions. She seemed to be very ill at ease in the luxury of his hotel. Rich heiresses were normally quite comfortable traveling well and rarely noted that they spent their time caring for others. It seemed there was another confusing layer to Paige. Was it possible that she'd been raised without the benefit of the family fortune?

"What do you do for a living?"

"I'm a registered nurse."

He couldn't suppress his groan at her response. That wasn't what he'd thought she would say. Everything about her surprised him.

"What's wrong with being a nurse?" she asked.

"Nothing is wrong with it. It's a noble calling. I've just spent more time than I ever wanted to around nurses. I was hospitalized for quite a long time with my injury. They were all great and cared for me very well, but I avoid hospitals at all costs now. I couldn't imagine working there every day."

"It's different when you're not the patient. I was a born caretaker. My mother told me I was such a little mama as a child. I was always carrying around my baby doll, and when I got older, I wanted to babysit at every opportunity. I thought maybe I would work in pediatrics one day. But when I spent time with my grandfather, he would tell me stories about

World War II. At least ones that were okay for a little girl to hear. It made me want to work with soldiers when I grew up, so that's what I did instead. I got a master's degree in nursing and I work at the veteran's hospital in San Diego on the orthopedic floor. I work mainly with soldiers that have lost limbs or had their joints replaced or rebuilt."

"That sounds like a hard job to have."

"It's difficult work, but it can be so rewarding. I love what I do. Almost all of my time goes to my job, which leaves little for me. I think that's why my grandfather wanted me to come here, to get a break."

Mano tried not to stiffen at Paige's words as she spoke about her work. It wasn't that there was anything wrong with her answer, but it did give him pause. Chuck had been right when he asked if Mano was considering Paige for more than just dinner. He'd only used it as an excuse to learn more about her. She'd caught his attention without even realizing it.

But knowing she was a nurse…that changed things.

She herself had said she was a caretaker. One of his aunts was a nurse. Since the day of his accident, she'd fawned over him, treating him as nearly helpless. People who went into nursing had a strong desire to care for others. Mano didn't want to be taken care of. He didn't want to be fixed or babied, and he certainly didn't want to be pitied.

Then again, there was something about Paige that his body reacted to instantly. He didn't know what she looked like or anything other than the feel of her hand in his, but he wanted to know more. As the pieces of her history started to click together in his mind, he found himself more interested instead of less. Of course she was a nurse. That explained the rough hands after washing them dozens of times a day and the scent of hand sanitizer.

"My grandfather knew this is something I never would've done on my own," she continued, oblivious to his thoughts. "He wanted me to take a break and enjoy life, if for just a week. So I'm trying. I find it's easier to do in Hawaii than it is at home."

"Everything is easier in Hawaii. It's a state of mind." Mano considered his options for this evening and decided that he didn't mind if she was a nurse. So far, she'd let him take the lead, not once going out of her way to help him when he didn't need it. Being a nurse might not be all bad. If things worked out, maybe she could give him a sponge bath…

He suppressed a wicked grin and tried to focus on what to do next. He didn't want their evening together to end so soon. It was Saturday night, which meant that the resort fireworks show was starting soon. He could take Paige somewhere to watch it, but he knew that the best view on the property was from his own balcony. Typically, he didn't allow anyone into his sanctuary, but for some reason he was almost eager to invite Paige upstairs. He could offer her dessert and an amazing show. But would she accept?

"Do you like fireworks?" he asked.

# Three

Paige only thought her penthouse was the pinnacle of luxury. That was before she stepped into Mano's suite.

The whole space was very clean and modern. Every detail, from the industrial light fixtures overhead to the abstract paintings on the walls, exuded elegance and masculinity with a hard edge. The floors were seamless white marble, the couch was covered in buttery soft gray leather and the tables looked like sheets of glass floating in the air with only the slightest bit of metal supporting them. It was the kind of almost austere look that at first glance might seem plain, but in fact was extremely expensive.

There were no fussy elements, no flower arrangements or lace or knickknacks. Everything seemed perfectly placed, as though an interior designer had handled each detail down to where the dog's leash hung on the wall. She supposed that things being out of place could cause a problem when you couldn't see to track down errant items.

There wasn't much for Paige to break, but what was there, she could tell, was fragile. She was anxious about being in Mano's suite for dozens of reasons, but now that she was here, she added the new worry of being someplace where she could stumble and put her fist through a priceless Jackson Pollock painting.

It had been hard enough for her to shake the surreal feeling as she followed him upstairs without those other worries. She wasn't really sure why she was here, anyway. She understood the polite dinner invitation, but why ask her to join him in his suite for dessert just to be nice to a lonely hotel guest? Maybe her initial reaction to their dinner date was closer to the truth and this was about more than just treating the VIPs.

Mano removed Hōkū's harness and the dog trotted over to his corner pillow where a rawhide bone was waiting for him. "We do fireworks at the hotel every Saturday night," Mano explained as he slipped out of his suit coat and laid it over the back of a chair that he seemed to know would be positioned just there. "It's a long-standing tradition at the Mau Loa that my grandparents started decades ago. My suite has one of the best views, ironically enough."

Paige bit at her lip as he noted the obvious issue. She followed him out onto the balcony and he was right—his view was even better than hers. The fireworks over the lagoon would be center stage for the spectators waiting along Waikiki beach, but their view had it all beat. "It's a shame you can't enjoy them."

"Actually, I can," Mano said as he gripped the railing and looked out over the water as though he could see it.

The moonlight highlighted the sharp angles of his face, reminding Paige just how handsome and unobtainable a man he was. She wished he would take off his glasses so she could see his eyes. She understood why he wore the glasses, but she felt like a part of him was hiding behind them.

"I remember what they looked like when I was younger. As I mentioned earlier, I didn't lose my eyesight until I was seventeen, so I have the memories. I can sit on my patio and listen to the pop of the fireworks and the cheers of the crowd. The smell of the smoke in the air brings back the experience for me. I don't need to see them anymore."

The doorbell of the suite rang just then, robbing Paige of any questions she might want to ask. With her medical background, she was curious about what had happened to him, but she needed the right opportunity to bring it up. She didn't want to pry, but she knew from her experience with soldiers that they often wanted to tell their story, but only when they were ready.

"Dessert has arrived," Mano said.

"I'll go get the door," Paige replied, beating him to the sliding door. He was able-bodied but so was she, so there was no reason why she couldn't let room service in for them.

At the door, a man was waiting with a cart. On top of it was a large silver-domed dish like the kind you'd see in old movies. "Good evening, ma'am. Where would you like your dessert?"

"Bring it out to the balcony, please," Mano called. He'd followed her into the living room even though he didn't need to.

They both trailed the cart back to the patio, where the waiter placed it on the glass table. "The famous Mau Loa Black Pearl," he announced, raising the lid with dramatic flair.

Paige couldn't help the gasp that escaped her lips when she saw the beautiful chocolate delight hidden beneath the silver dome. Mano had told her it was the showpiece of The Pearl, and the dessert looked exactly like a giant black pearl in an oyster. A thin hinged cookie shell was the bed and backdrop for a dome of layered chocolate mousse. It was enrobed in a dark chocolate fudge ganache and dusted with toasted coconut and macadamia nuts on the edges. It was the most beautiful and delicious-looking thing she'd ever seen in her life.

"I don't think I can eat it," she said.

Mano chuckled as he gave the waiter his tip and he disappeared from the suite. "You'll change your mind about that pretty quickly. It's the most incredible thing you'll ever put in your mouth."

They sat down in the patio chairs and armed themselves with spoons. Mano broke through the dark chocolate outside first so Paige didn't have to do it. One bite and she knew he was right. The different layers and flavors of chocolate mousse and cream melted together on her tongue. The decorative starburst of passion fruit puree on the plate gave a sharp sour bite to break up the richness. The cookie was crunchy, almost like a fortune cookie, but much more flavorful. It was amazing. And gone before they knew it.

"That was incredible," Paige said as she laid her spoon down on the empty plate. "I think I might burst, though."

"It will be worth any suffering." Mano paused for a moment, putting his hand to the tiny headset that always seemed to be in his ear. "Ah, perfect timing. The fireworks show is about to start. Are you ready?" He held out his hand to her.

Paige took it and they walked together to the railing. Heavy drums and traditional Hawaiian music sounded from the lagoon in the distance. A moment later, the sky lit up as a firework exploded and bathed the darkness in streaks of white fire. One after the next, bursts of color danced across the sky. For about ten minutes it continued, illuminating the dark water. Down below, she could hear the crowds gathered on the beach as they cheered and gasped in awe.

"That was wonderful," Paige said as the last of the smoke started to clear. "You were right, you do have the best view for the show."

"I'm glad you enjoyed it."

Paige turned away from the beach to look at him. "I want to thank you for all this."

He shrugged it away. "It's nothing."

"No, it's not nothing. You've taken me to a lovely dinner, brought me up here for an amazing dessert and fireworks. You've saved me from a lonely night in a beautiful place. That's more than other people would've done for a stranger. More than other people typically do for me."

Mano's brow furrowed as he listened to her. "What do you mean? Do the people in your life back at home take advantage of your kindness?"

Paige sighed and leaned onto the railing. "It isn't that simple." She wasn't bullied or abused at all. She just didn't quite fit in. It was mostly a case of being invisible. "More often than not, I'm just ignored.

No one really seems to see me. I just blend into the background noise no matter how loud I yell. Sometimes I wonder if, when I die, anyone will even remember I existed."

"Your patients will remember you. I know I'll never forget the kind nurses that cared for me after my accident."

"I hope you're right," Paige said. She tried to make a difference in their lives, even when it didn't seem like she was getting anywhere.

Mano's hand slid along the railing until he found hers. He covered her with his reassuring warmth. "And I'll remember you, Paige Edwards."

Her breath caught in her throat at his words and his caress. Her skin seemed to sing beneath his touch. A thrill ran up her arm and jolted her heart to beat double time in her chest. She knew she shouldn't get excited. Mano wasn't putting the moves on her; he was being kind. And yet, her body didn't seem to know the difference. "I'll remember you, too. You are the first person in a long time that truly seems to see me."

"Sometimes people depend too much on their eyes," Mano explained. "They make all their judgments based on what they see, ignoring everything else. I may not know what you look like, Paige, but I know a lot of other things about you that make you a person I want to know more about."

She really couldn't understand why he felt that

way. She was a nobody—certainly not the kind of woman who captured the attention of a rich, handsome man like Mano. "I don't know what you see that others don't. Frankly, I don't even see it. I've never thought I was very special."

"That's odd," Mano said. "I find myself wanting to know everything about you. It seems I uncover a surprise with every layer I peel away. May I ask you something?"

Paige shifted nervously, pulling back from his touch. Usually when someone prefaced a question like that, it was going to be bad. Like when her sister asked if Paige's relationship with Wyatt was really serious. She was just testing the waters before she jumped in. "Why not?" she said at last. After what she'd been through lately, there wasn't much he could ask that would make things worse.

"May I touch your face?"

Except for maybe that.

"I know that sounds odd," Mano continued, "but it's how I see people. I'd like to see you better."

A part of Paige was happy that Mano couldn't see her. He seemed so interested in her. Would finding out how she looked ruin their perfect night together? She supposed that telling him no would end it just as awkwardly. "Okay," she agreed.

Mano turned to face her, but his expression was as concerned as hers likely appeared. "You sound nervous. You don't have to do it if you don't want to."

"No, it's okay," she argued, placing a hand on his forearm. "If you had your sight, you would've known what I looked like from the first moment, so you've waited long enough to know. I just hope you're not disappointed with what you find."

Disappointed? Most of the women who had drifted in and out of Mano's life had a healthy sense of self-esteem, but not Paige. Whether or not she was right, she seemed to think she was invisible or even unattractive. He didn't think that was actually possible, but now he'd find out for himself.

Taking her wrists in his hands, he let his palms glide up her arms to her neck. There, he cradled her face in his hands. Paige was tense and still beneath his fingertips as they traced the lines and angles of her face. She had a delicate brow, large, wide eyes and a sharp nose. Her face was thin, as was the rest of her, judging by her narrow wrists and protruding collar bones.

He realized then that she was too still and too silent beneath his touch. "Breathe, Paige."

She moved slightly with a sudden exhale and intake of breath. Once she relaxed, his fingers ran over her hair. It was long, straight and silky. Paige hadn't twisted it up or tortured it with curling irons and hair spray. It just flowed naturally down her back.

"What color are your eyes?" he asked, trying to envision them in his mind.

"They're a hazel color. Not quite green and not quite brown."

Mano nodded, the picture coming together. "Now, tell me about what you're wearing tonight so I can see it."

"I overdressed a little," she confessed. "It's a blue satin cocktail dress that I found on sale at the mall. I don't even know why I bought it—I have nowhere to wear it normally—but I threw it into the suitcase when I was packing. I figured if I didn't wear it tonight, I might as well donate it to charity."

He didn't know why she had to cut herself down with every description of herself. "What shade of blue?"

"A dark royal blue, kind of like the deeper waters off Waikiki."

Mano could see that color vividly in his memory. He wished he could continue his exploration, run his hands over her body to find out more about her. Feeling bold, he traced the neckline of the gown with his finger, finding the V plunged deep. His fingertip lingered at the apex for a moment as Paige let out a ragged breath. He expected her to pull away or tell him to stop, but she didn't. She leaned closer to him. The scent of her mingled with the Plumeria and orchids that perfumed the breezes. He was intoxicated by it and drawn to her in a way he simply didn't understand.

Gently cupping her face in his hands, he lowered

his lips to hers. Her response to him was cautious, but curious. After a moment, the caution gave way to enthusiasm. She wrapped her arms around his neck and arched her body against him. Mano felt his every muscle tighten as her lithe body pressed into his own.

He let his tongue explore her mouth as his hands explored her body. She had the taste of decadent chocolate lingering on her lips. Her body was lean and angular to the touch, with few curves to cup in his hands. Considering how tiny she'd felt when he'd touched her earlier, he wasn't surprised. It was just another way that his Paige was different.

As his hand strayed near her belly, she went stiff as stone in his arms. "Paige?"

He felt her pull away and the next thing he knew, her loud and unsteady clomp of heels against the marble floors grew softer and softer until the front door of his suite slammed shut. She'd just run away.

He'd had a lot of reactions to his kisses in his life, but he'd never had a woman turn tail and run. For a moment, Mano wasn't exactly sure what to do, but in the end, he decided to give chase. He wasn't going to let Paige run away from this. If nothing else, he would apologize for crossing a line and making her uncomfortable, but he felt like it was more than that.

Mano made his way cautiously through the suite to the entrance, then across the vestibule to Paige's door. He pressed the doorbell of her suite and waited as patiently as he could. His heart was still pounding in his chest and his muscles were still tight with tension from their kiss. It was possible that Paige just wouldn't answer the door, but he didn't think she was the kind to just ignore him. That would be impolite.

Mano heard her soft shoeless footsteps approach the door and it unlatched with a metallic pop. The door swung open.

"Yes?"

He could tell by the harsh tone of her voice that she was upset. Mano just wasn't sure if she was upset with him or herself. "Did I do something wrong?" he asked.

"No. You were wonderful. Everything I could've asked for and more on a night out in the most romantic place in the world. It's just me. I'm sorry," she said.

And here he thought he'd been the one apologizing. "Sorry for what?"

"For everything," she said with a sadness in her voice that told of more than just tonight's worries on her mind. "For kissing you, then for running. In the moment, I wasn't really sure what to do. I don't trust myself when it comes to these things. I make poor decisions, and I'm not saying that kissing you is a mistake, but I'm really not at a place in my life where I need this kind of...complication."

Complication? Paige seemed to have tied herself

up in knots for no reason. He could feel the anxiety and tension damn near radiating from her body in waves. "It was just a kiss, Paige. There's no need to make more of it than that. How complicated can things get with you leaving in less than a week?"

He reached out for her and placed a hand on her waist. He waited until she relaxed and the throbbing pulse beneath his fingertips slowed. "Listen, Paige, I want you to know this isn't something I do very often. I've never even invited a guest up to my suite before."

"Really?"

"Really." It was true. Only Chuck, housekeeping and room service were allowed inside from the hotel staff. When he did indulge in a short romance, he always went to the woman's room or sought out an empty suite. And yet, he'd wanted to share his retreat with Paige. He wanted to experience those fireworks with her, knowing it would be as though he could see them again. "Like you, I don't really trust myself in relationships, either. My condition puts me at a disadvantage. Every time I'm with a woman, I wonder what her angle is, or if I'll be a burden on her. To be honest, your work as a nurse is a huge red flag for me. I should walk away from you right now."

"Why?"

"Because I don't want to be someone's project. I can't be fixed and I don't want to be coddled. Some women see me as someone they can care for and, as a nurse, it's in your nature to do it."

Paige chuckled softly. "You'll find that I'm more drill sergeant than babysitter. Sometimes it takes a firm hand to get a patient out of bed and make him stop feeling sorry for himself."

"Maybe that's the difference. There's just something about you that makes me want to throw all my rules out the window. I want to know more about you, Paige. I want to touch you again."

Paige gasped. He took a step closer to her and drew her hand to his chest. "I don't want to make you uncomfortable. If you tell me to, I'll walk away right now and leave you alone for the rest of your time here in Hawaii. But I don't want to. Whatever we share doesn't have to be serious or complicated, Paige. I'm proposing we spend the week together. I'll let you set the boundaries so there's no unwanted complications. I simply enjoy your company."

"You do?"

Her voice was soft and small, so insecure it made his chest ache. What had Paige been through that she thought so little of herself? She questioned his every interest in her. "I absolutely do. I don't know why every man you meet doesn't feel the same way. You're charming, thoughtful and kind."

Paige laughed softly, but he could tell it wasn't with amusement but with disbelief. "You're the first person to ever say that. The people that don't ignore me entirely find me to be awkward and quiet. I don't know exactly what it is that a man like you sees in a woman like me."

Mano frowned. "What kind of man am I?"

He felt her shrug. "I don't know…handsome, wealthy, successful… The kind that could have a dozen supermodels in his contact list if he wanted to. That kind of man doesn't really belong with a woman like me."

"Supermodels aren't much for interesting conversation. I have different priorities. I might be blind, Paige, but I see more than most because I rely on more than just my eyes. What I see of you, I like. So, will I see you tomorrow?" he asked.

After a moment's hesitation she said, "I'll think about it."

Mano smiled and took a step back from her doorway. "You do that. When you decide to accept my proposal, and you will, just ask any hotel employee for me and I'll find you. Good night, Paige."

As he reached the doorway of his room, he heard Paige's door click shut behind him. Inside his suite, he went to the kitchen and sought out a bottle of locally brewed beer. Sinking into his leather couch, he took a sip and hoped that the muscles in his body could uncurl with the help of the alcohol.

Hōkū trotted over to the sofa and jumped up beside him. He laid his heavy head onto Mano's lap and sighed. That was pretty much how he felt, too.

He wasn't sure if Paige would take him up on his offer to spend time together or not. He hoped so, but nothing was certain.

Since his accident, Mano had become very distrusting of women. Before, when he was the vibrant younger Bishop brother with everything ahead of him, he liked it when the girls swarmed him. Even then, he only had eyes for Jenna. He had been dating her since their sophomore year, and they had everything going for them. Like his older brother, Kal, he was about to graduate and go on to the University of Hawaii. He and Jenna had plans to take over the family business with his brother and branch out to new locations, turning the Mau Loa into the most luxurious hotel chain in the islands. First Maui, then Kauai. He was young, rich, handsome and soon to be very powerful. He felt invincible with her at his side.

Then, in the blink of an eye, everything changed. On the way to his brother's football game an oncoming SUV strayed from its lane and plowed head-on into his parents' car at fifty miles an hour. Their parents were killed on impact. Mano hit his head with enough force to blind him permanently, break his arm and earn about twenty stitches across his brow.

Suddenly, he wasn't the golden child he always thought he'd be. Recovering from his accident had been a challenge. Kal and their grandparents tried to convince him that he'd only lost his vision, not his life, but Mano knew better. Even the girls around him knew better. Jenna disappeared, carrying on with her plans and leaving him behind. She said she was too young to dedicate her whole life to loving a man with a lifetime of challenges ahead of him. Suddenly, he went from being a catch to a charity case.

Over the last ten years, Mano had managed by only allowing himself the physical comforts of a relationship—nothing emotional. A week with a woman every few months or so was enough to soothe the beast. He didn't want or expect anything more than that.

He certainly looked forward to a week with Paige. *If* she agreed to it.

A buzz of conversation in Mano's ear distracted him from his thoughts. There was an issue downstairs that he needed to tend to. Giving Hōkū a pat on the head, he took one last sip of his beer and left the rest to go flat on the coffee table. He sought out his suit coat and Hōkū's harness, preparing to head back downstairs.

Thankfully, work was always there to distract him from everything, including his own life.

# Four

Mano didn't sleep well. Being completely blind, he usually had some level of difficulty because he didn't have the light cues to regulate his circadian rhythm. Medication usually helped, but not last night. Though last night had less to do with being blind and more to do with Paige.

He'd tossed and turned thinking about that kiss. Her eagerness countered by her quick retreat was a beautiful collision of contradictions. She'd called what happened between them last night "a complication." He hoped he was able to convince her otherwise. She would only be on Oahu for a few days, but he wanted to take advantage of every moment he could with her. He wanted to taste her lips again and feel her body press against his. He wanted to ask her more questions because she surprised him with every answer.

His brain had circled around those thoughts until the wee hours when he finally fell asleep. The morning alarm came early. Hōkū didn't really care that he hadn't slept. He was ready to go outside, so down they went. Mano grabbed a latte with a double shot from the coffee shop on their way back upstairs so he could wake up and get ready for work.

Mano was stepping out of the shower when he heard the doorbell. Hōkū barked and stood anxious at the door as he slipped into his robe and made his way to answer it. He couldn't fathom who would be at the door at this hour. It was too early for him to even have his earpiece in yet.

Tightening the belt around his waist, he asked through the door, "Who is it?"

"It's Paige," a soft voice answered back.

Without really considering that he was wearing nothing more than a robe, Mano whipped open the door. He didn't know why Paige was on his doorstep at dawn, but he wanted to find out immediately.

A muffled gasp was her response. Mano adjusted the wrap of the robe around him to make sure he wasn't exposing anything and ran his hand self-consciously through the wet strands of his hair. "Is everything okay?" he asked.

"Y-yes," she stammered. "I'm sorry to come by

at such a miserable hour. You're obviously still getting ready. I haven't adjusted to the time change and I just uh… I wanted to catch you before you went to work. I wanted to see if you'd be interested in playing hooky with me today."

"Hooky, *pulelehua*?"

"Yes, that's why I came by when I did. Last night you said you wanted to spend some more time with me. You proposed a week together in the most romantic place on earth. I said I would think about it and I did. All night, actually. And I've decided that if you want to spend these few days with me, I'm not going to be the one to turn you away."

A wide smile spread across Mano's face. When he'd left her last night, he hadn't been certain of Paige's answer. In his mind, she seemed like a skittish doe that would flee at any sudden movements. But now his doe was getting bolder. "I'm glad to hear that."

"I thought that we could spend the day out. I mean, it's a Sunday, after all, and you own the place. You could take the day off without asking permission, right?"

Mano's brow furrowed in thought. "I don't know. I don't usually leave the property. This is a little short notice for my staff."

She didn't bother to disagree with him. Her silence spoke volumes. He supposed she was right. He could leave, he simply never did it. His world completely revolved around the Mau Loa, and mostly by his own design. Nothing required him to be there, on call, twenty-four hours a day. He could have a home he returned to each night instead of converting one of the penthouse suites into his private apartment. He could take vacations and sick days the same as every other employee on site did. He simply didn't do it. Mano couldn't think of the last time he'd taken a day off.

"It'll be fun," she encouraged with a musical lilt to her voice. "Come on, Mano. Show me everything your beautiful island has to offer. I may never come back. I've got to make the most of every minute."

"You absolutely should. I can make some great recommendations—"

"No, I want *you* to show me Oahu. You can't spend all your time in this hotel, Mano. There's a whole island outside your property lines, and I want us to see it together."

"I don't spend all my time in the hotel," he argued, knowing it was a lie. He only made the occasional trip to Maui to see Kal. What was he going to do? Go sightseeing? Snorkel? That was kind of pointless.

"Sure you don't." Paige sounded anything but convinced. "What was the last thing you did outside the resort?"

Mano couldn't answer that question. He had no clue. His groceries were delivered. Most of his other needs were handled at the hotel. He had his assistant order whatever he needed online. His last trip out might have been to the tailor to get some suits fitted the year before last, but he certainly wasn't going to admit that. Instead, he pushed up his sleeves and raised his hands in defeat. "Okay, you win. You really are a bit of a drill sergeant. Hooky it is." He took a step back from the door. "Please, come in. I'll go put some clothes on."

"You don't have to—I mean, put clothes on. That didn't come out right. I'm not asking you to *not* put clothes on. I just meant that I can wait until you're dressed. You don't have to invite me in. Take whatever time you need."

Mano did his best not to laugh. Paige had the ability to get twisted in her own words in the most endearing way. It was charming. Of course, he wasn't helping the matter by opening the door fresh from the shower. In this robe, it was likely that she could see his native tattoos and his scars, two things he usually kept hidden beneath his Armani armor. Hell, he hadn't even remembered to put on his sunglasses before he answered the door. She just seemed to have thrown him off balance last night and he had yet to recover, making one mistake after the next.

Paige sighed heavily. "I'll wait outside," she said.

"Okay. Just give me a few minutes."

Mano closed the door and headed back to his bedroom. He wasn't entirely sure what to wear for a day of fun on his island home. It had been a long time since he'd even tried. He started by picking up his earpiece from the charging station beside the bed.

"This is Mr. Bishop. Who's listening?"

"Good morning, Mr. Bishop," a man's voice responded. "This is Duke. What can I do for you?"

Duke was the night shift operations manager, second in command to Chuck. "Morning, Duke. Would you let Chuck know when he gets here that I won't be in today?"

There was a long hesitation. "Are you unwell? Should I have the resort doctor sent up to your suite, sir?"

He did need to get out more. "No, Duke, I'm fine. I'm just taking the day off."

"Very well. I'll let him know, sir."

Mano took off the headset and put it back on the dresser. It felt weird not to leave it on, as he did every day, but it wouldn't work once he left the resort. And today, that was apparently what he was doing.

Reaching into the bottom drawer of his dresser, he pulled out cargo shorts and a polo shirt. He added his only pair of flip-flops. He wasn't sure which color polo he was wearing, but he knew his flip-flops were brown and would go with anything. With that handled, he returned to the bathroom to finish grooming and drying his hair. Feeling carefree, he skipped shaving. He always shaved, but if he was going to play hooky today, he was going all out.

The last thing he did before reopening the door was slip the harness onto Hōkū and his glasses over his eyes. When he reopened the door, he called out to see if Paige was still waiting for him. "Paige?"

"I'm right here." He heard the opposite door shut and listened to her steps as she approached him. "I wanted to grab a few last things before we left. I'm not sure what we'll do today, but I figured my sunglasses and my camera were a must. Are you ready to go?"

Mano nodded. "Yep." He held his arm out to her and once she slipped hers through it and snuggled beside him, they went to the elevator.

After he pressed the button she asked, "So, what *are* we going to do today?"

That was a good question. He'd just come to terms with the idea of "hooky" so he hadn't fully developed today's itinerary. Normally, he handed guests a couple brochures from the display by the concierge desk and sent them on their way. But what would he do if he was going along? That might be a little different. For one thing, he was hungry. "I was thinking we'd start with pancakes."

"Pancakes?"

Mano nodded. "Every decent day of hooky needs to start with an indulgent breakfast. I recommend we go to Eggs 'n Things for macadamia nut pancakes with coconut syrup and whipped butter. There's a lot of pancake houses around the island, but this one was my favorite as a kid. I haven't been there in ages."

"Those pancakes sound wonderful," she said with a smile in her voice.

The doors of the elevator opened and they stepped in together to start their day's journey.

Paige was exhausted and she was pretty sure she had the start of a sunburn, even though she'd put on sunblock, but she didn't care. She was having too much fun with Mano and they hadn't even strayed from the Waikiki Beach area yet.

They started out with pancakes, then they continued to stroll down the main path that snaked around the beach. Mano took her hand as they walked. It was probably just so he didn't lose her in the crowds, but the feel of her hand in his made a shiver run down her spine. Although she was a tall, lanky woman, she felt petite and feminine beside Mano. She rarely felt like either of those things.

They went through the narrow aisles of an open air market, where she was nearly overwhelmed by vendor after vendor selling every type of souvenir she could think of. Mano and Hōkū were remarkably patient as she looked at things they'd been surrounded by their whole lives. He explained different items they had for sale and helped her negotiate a better deal on a few things. She picked up something for her parents and something for her best friend, Brandy. Brandy was a nurse on her shift at the veteran's hospital and one of the few she could call a friend.

Somehow her work environment had evolved into a sorority house, with veterans hanging around instead of football players. The other nurses weren't necessarily mean, but she wouldn't call any of them friends, either. Paige had never been very good at fitting in, no matter what she was trying to do. Even now, she was getting odd glances from people as they passed, trying to figure out the two of them together.

Fortunately, she didn't have to try to fit in with Mano, so she could ignore everyone else. He seemed to find her differences charming, although she really didn't understand why. He laughed at her jokes, held her hand and looked as proud to be with her as if he was with a famous Hollywood actress. She almost didn't know how to act around him. The last guy she met who was this charming was just using her, but Mano seemed totally sincere. He'd given up a whole day at work to spend time with her, after all, with no promise of anything in return.

It was late in the afternoon when she spied a Hawaiian shaved ice place and begged to go inside. He bought them each a huge snowball of sugar and ice and they found a table under a shady palm tree where they could eat and Paige could watch the ocean.

"It's been a long time since I've had one of these," he admitted as he took his first few bites. "My mother used to take me and my brother down to the beach and buy us one from time to time. It's as good as I remember. I wonder if I should put in a Hawaiian ice place at the hotel."

"You absolutely should." She took a bite of her Tiger's Blood flavored ice and let it melt on her tongue. "Maybe near the big pool so people can get a cool treat while they're enjoying the sun. Honestly, I can't believe you don't have one already."

Mano shrugged. "Well, when my grandparents opened the hotel, Waikiki was a different place. It wasn't long before it exploded into an endless strip of hotels and gift shops. There were more US soldiers than tourists back then. Hell, Hawaii wasn't even a state yet. Their goal was first and foremost to have the most authentic, yet luxurious, experience for guests. The resort grew and expanded over time under my family's watchful eyes, just as Honolulu grew and changed. When it was handed over to me, I was mindful to make sure that my grandfather would approve of anything I did. My grandparents are still alive, so my whole life I've gotten an earful about the tacky and cheap things other resorts are doing every time I go to visit them."

Paige understood those family expectations. She

supposed she failed in most areas, while her sister, Piper, excelled. That was okay with her, though. Her patients loved her and that was more important to her. "I am certain you can open up the classiest shaved ice shop on the whole island."

They chuckled as they sat together and finished their frozen treats. As Paige set her cup aside, she noticed the tattoo on Mano's left forearm again. This time she had a much better view of the design. It was simple and geometrical, with rings of black triangles encircling his forearm. She'd never seen a tattoo like it before.

"What does your tattoo mean?"

She watched as Mano self-consciously ran his palm over the black ink etched into his forearm. "This is a traditional Hawaiian tattoo. These triangles symbolize a shark's teeth. My parents named me after the Hawaiian word for shark because my grandmother had a dream of me swimming with sharks while my mother was pregnant. It's considered to be my spirit animal. My people also believe that if I were to run across a shark in the ocean, it would see the tattoo and recognize me as kindred."

Paige reached out and traced along the rows of triangles that went from just below his elbow to his wrist. She could see the line of a scar hidden beneath the ink. It was probably the companion scar to the one on his brow and the smaller spatter of scars she'd seen on his chest that morning. She noticed that Mano stiffened under her touch and a ragged breath escaped his lips. Instantly, she forgot all about the tattoo and was focused entirely on the beautiful man it belonged to.

It was nice to sit so still and close to him. His skin was warm to the touch from the sun and when the breeze blew just right, she got a whiff of his scent. It was something earthy and masculine like sandalwood and leather. It made her want to lean closer and press her nose against the line of his throat to draw it fully into her lungs. As much as she was tempted, Paige resisted. Instead, she studied the interesting lines and angles of his face without worrying that he would notice her staring.

He had such an interesting face. The scar across his brow and the flat distortion of his nose could be considered flaws to some, but it gave him so much character. He had his glasses on now, but that morning, she'd gotten her first glimpse of his eyes. They had been more striking than even the sight of his bare chest. They were a dark brown that seemed to see right through her despite their lack of focus. She could just imagine those eyes looking at her through the dark lenses. She could watch him like this for hours.

Well, at least until he mentioned the awkward silence between them. "What?" he asked, turning to look in her direction.

"Nothing," she said as she cleared her throat and

turned her attention back to his muscular and inked forearm. "It's just such a beautiful piece."

That made Mano smile. "I'm glad you think so. It's almost a rite of passage for the men in my family to receive their tattoo. I went through almost nine hours of traditional Hawaiian tapping to have it done. I'd like to think it was worth it, although I've never seen the results, myself."

Paige was surprised, although she supposed she shouldn't be. He'd mentioned losing his vision as a teenager, so if he'd gotten the tattoo as an adult, he wouldn't have seen it. "That's a lot of pain to protect yourself from sharks when you never get into the ocean."

Mano nodded softly and pulled his arm away from her touch. He ran his hand hard over the skin, almost scrubbing away her touch, before moving it out of her sight. "There are plenty of sharks to be wary of on land, as well."

She certainly knew that to be true. She wished the music from *Jaws* had played when Wyatt started circling her. Maybe then she wouldn't be in the predicament she was in—a predicament she still hadn't confided in Mano about. She wondered if it would really matter to him. They had a week together, not a lifetime. He'd likely never even know if she didn't bring it up. Yet at the same time, the grave seriousness with which he'd just spoken was the voice of experience. She didn't know everything he'd struggled through in his life, but she would do her best not to add to it. She should definitely tell him about the baby. At least before things got any more serious.

Paige turned to the ocean, searching for a way to mention it before they got too close. Instead, she caught a glimpse of a pod of dolphins buzzing past a few surfers. "Oh!" she cried out, gripping Mano's arm.

"What?" he asked with an edge of panic in his voice. Mano came across much more confident at the resort than he was out with her today. Being unable to see the world around him seemed to make him a little edgy. He must know every inch of the Mau Loa like the back of his hand, yet out here he was at a disadvantage.

"Nothing bad," she said soothingly. "Dolphins. There's about twelve or fifteen of them."

The tension disappeared from Mano's body. "Oh yeah. They're all over out here. It's too early in the season for the humpback whales, but spinner dolphins are here year-round. If you go out on the water while you're visiting, you'll get a chance to see them up close for sure. They like the wake of the boats."

That was an interesting idea. She hadn't given much thought to that yet. Including Mano in her plans had both enhanced and limited her options. He was a very capable man, but there were just some things that were either difficult or pointless when you couldn't see. But there were still options… "You know, I saw a brochure at the hotel for a dinner cruise that departs from the pier near the Mau Loa."

"It's a nice operation. I recommend it to a lot of hotel guests. Half of Hawaii is underwater. You've got to get out there or get in it to have the full island experience."

Snorkeling or kayaking with Mano might not be feasible, but Paige thought a dinner cruise was very doable. "What about tonight?"

"What about tonight, what?"

Paige frowned with a touch of irritation. "What about you and I take that dinner cruise tonight?"

"Hmm." It was a thoughtful yet noncommittal sound that nonetheless drew her attention to his full lips and made her more interested in kissing him again than going out on a boat. Of course, there was no reason why she couldn't do both. The dinner cruise might be romantic.

"Please?" she asked with a hint of begging in her voice.

Mano twisted his lips in thought then finally sighed in defeat. "Okay. I'll call the concierge and see if I can book for tonight. They fill up early sometimes, though, so don't get your heart set on it yet. We might have to go another day."

He pulled out his cell phone and Paige sat with baited breath while she listened to him complete the call. He asked several questions, all positive from her side of the conversation. In a few minutes he hung up and slipped the phone back into his pocket.

"You're one lucky lady, *pulelehua*. They just had a cancellation for tonight, and I confirmed that they're okay with service dogs on board."

"Yay!" Paige cheered and wrapped her arms around his neck. She startled him, but he quickly recovered by returning the embrace. His arms were warm and strong around her, the hard muscles of his chest pressing against her small breasts. She felt her body start to respond to the simple hug and began to pull back, but he wouldn't let go.

Instead, his lips met hers. It was an easy kiss, sweet but firm. His lips tasted like watermelon shaved ice and his tongue was still slightly cold against her own.

"Okay," he muttered against her lips as they came apart. Mano pressed a button on his watch, announcing the time aloud as just after four. "I think we'd better head back to the hotel. I don't think cargo shorts will meet the dinner dress code. And besides that, I think you need to put on more sunblock."

Paige sat back and looked down at her pinkening skin. "How do you know that?"

"Your skin is hot to the touch. Either you're sunburned or feverish."

Paige smiled. She was always amazed by how much he noticed when it seemed like he would miss most things. "How do you know I'm not just all warmed up from that kiss?"

Mano laughed and pushed back from the table. "It's possible, but if you get that hot from a simple kiss, you're going to be in trouble later."

# Five

Mano couldn't remember how long it had been since he'd gotten on a boat. He might have been on one catamaran since the accident. Kal had made him do it, but that had been enough for him. The charter to Lanai from Maui was on choppy seas and he'd clung to the railing for dear life. It had seemed like a stupid thing for a blind man to do.

Kal was never really interested in acknowledging Mano's limitations. He tried to stay positive about the whole thing, insisting that Mano could do anything he wanted to do. His brother didn't like the idea of him being trapped inside the Mau Loa. Paige favored his brother a lot in that way. He supposed it was her work with veterans. They overcame disabilities every day. Why should Mano be any different?

Because he *was* different. He'd learned to function as well as possible in the world he knew now. Part of that was knowing his limitations.

As Hōkū led them up the ramp to the dinner yacht, Mano hoped he wasn't making a mistake. It was hard to say no to Paige, though. It was just a dinner cruise around the south side of the island. The boat likely had stabilizers to keep them from rocking everywhere or guests might end up wearing their dinner instead of eating it.

"Thank you for doing this. I know it isn't your first choice for a way to spend the evening."

Mano pushed aside his doubts and tried to give her his most confident smile. "I don't have to steer the boat, so we should be fine. To be honest, I've always wanted to try the cruise, but I figured the view would be lackluster."

"Very funny."

"Well, it's true. The company makes up for it, however."

"Mr. Bishop," a man's voice greeted them as they neared the deck. "Thank you for joining us tonight. Just take one big step up, sir, and you'll be secure on the ship."

Mano sensed Hōkū move ahead of him and felt out his step before climbing onto the boat with Paige at his side.

"If you'll come right this way, I'll show you to our rear deck where we're serving wine and canapés."

They followed the host around the ship, where they were greeted with their choice of beverages and some small bites to tide them over until dinner. Paige opted for sparkling water once again and this time, he opted for the same. Alcohol seemed a poor choice given the situation.

Mano held Paige tight at his side as they mingled with other guests on the cruise. Everyone seemed enamored with Hōkū, who basked in the praise. Mano was far more interested in the bare skin he ran across when his palm came to rest on Paige's lower back. His fingers felt around, casually searching for fabric, and found the silky edge just shy of indecency. Moving up, he realized she hadn't worn a bra tonight, either. Her back was one bare expanse of skin. The realization made his blood hum in his veins, and he wished dinner would go ahead and start so it would end. He was far more interested in getting her back to his hotel suite.

When they were finally shown to their table, he was happy to find they were at a private table for two. He would rather talk to Paige alone than continue the small talk. She read the menu choices to him since a braille menu wasn't available and they gave their selections to the waiter.

"Is the table nice?" he asked once the server was gone.

"Oh yes," Paige said. "Our table is right at the

window so we have the best view of the water. The sun is just starting to set."

Mano nodded. "Sounds nice. What about you? How do you look tonight?"

"Well," Paige began thoughtfully, "I think I pale in comparison to an Oahu sunset, but I tried."

"I don't know," Mano said thoughtfully. "I felt a whole lot of skin earlier. I'm envisioning you in something pretty slinky."

"I'm wearing a halter gown. It ties around my neck and it's open in the back. It hangs fairly loosely to the ground."

"What color is it?"

"Red."

"I like it. What shade of red?"

"A dark red. Not quite burgundy. I'm just now noticing how it's highlighting the sun I got today. I probably look like a lobster."

"Stop it, Paige," he said softly but firmly. He didn't understand why she always cut herself down. A lot of women were prone to dismissing compliments, but she took it a step further. She didn't seem to think very highly of herself at all, and that was a damn shame. Here he was envisioning her in a sexy red dress and she thought she looked like a boiled crustacean.

"Stop what?" she asked.

She cut herself down so easily, she didn't even know she was doing it. Reaching across the table, he sought out her face with his hand. "Don't pull away," he insisted and finally felt her cheek against his palm. "I've spent enough time with you, Paige, to know you are a beautiful woman, inside and out."

"You don't know anything," she said flatly.

"Don't I? I've touched your face, kissed your lips, held your body... I've drawn the scent of you into my lungs and tasted you on my tongue. I've heard your soft sighs and melodic laughter. I don't need eyes to see you, Paige. Every word out of your mouth convinces me more and more how lovely you are. It pains me to hear you insist otherwise."

The silence answered him back. He withdrew his hand and waited for her response.

When it finally came it was quiet, nearly a whisper. "You're right. Thank you."

It wasn't very convincing, but it was a start. They might only be spending a week together, but he wanted Paige to return to the mainland feeling like a million bucks. It wasn't normally his style to double as lover and therapist, but he'd never met a woman so...broken before. She had no reason to be. He was the broken one, and he had more confidence in his little finger than she had in her whole body. It simply wasn't right, and he was determined to fix it.

At the same time, he started to regret chastising her on their evening out. Whether or not what he said was true, it seemed to quiet her. Their dinner went by with him trying to make conversation and her giving as many one word responses as she could muster. It was nearly painful. When the crew announced that there would be dancing and live music on the upper deck, he jumped at the chance.

"Would you like to dance, *pulelehua*?"

More silence. "I'm not a very good dancer," she said at last.

"That's okay. I can't see how bad you are."

That earned a chuckle out of her. "All right. What about Hōkū?"

"He has four left feet. We'll leave him to the side for a little while."

He took her hand and he let her lead them around the ship to the stairs and up to the main deck. There, the warm breeze ruffled his hair even as he could feel the night start to cool with the setting of the sun.

One of the servers offered to attend to Hōkū, so Mano passed off his lead and followed Paige onto the dance floor. The band was playing something a little jazzy and slow. He slipped one arm behind her back and took her hand in his. They rocked in a slow, easy motion to the music. He could feel the hesitation in Paige's every step, but after a few minutes, she finally relaxed against him.

"This isn't so bad, is it?" he asked.

"No," Paige admitted. "It's nice. I've never really slow danced with a man before."

"Really?" Mano didn't know why he was surprised after all she'd told him, but he was. "Not even in high school?"

"Definitely not in high school. I wasn't very popular. What about you?"

"I was very popular," Mano said. "All the girls loved me. And I loved them. Things were going great for me in that department until the accident."

"Did the girls really walk away from you when you lost your vision?" She sounded aghast at the mere idea.

"Some," Mano said. One in particular, but he wasn't in the mood to tell her about Jenna. He'd rather Paige think he was a playboy than a broken-hearted teenage boy who lost almost everything he loved in a single moment. "I think I pushed most of them away. I was so angry for so long that I hardly wanted to be around myself. I don't blame them for taking a step back."

"I see that a lot in my patients," Paige said. "So many of them intended to be soldiers for life. It was what they felt they were made to do. Then some IED blows their arms off and they're shipped home to live a life they never envisioned. It's hard on them. A lot of them don't adjust well. I spend a lot of my time not only helping them heal physically, but emotionally. Too many walk out the door and put a bullet through their head. But if you can get through to them, they can really live a full life. They have to make adjustments, but they can still do anything they put their mind to."

"Do you really believe that?" Mano asked.

"I do. I've seen it happen. Determination can take you far. I mean, look at you. You run that hotel like a well-oiled machine. It's amazing. I have no doubt that if you wanted to take on some new challenge, you'd succeed."

"You remind me of my brother."

"Is that a bad thing?"

"Not entirely. Only when he's pestering the snot out of me. He was always very positive about how I could still lead the life I wanted to lead after the accident. I've never been as certain. I think for him, it was mostly guilt. He wanted me to do everything I'd wanted to so he wouldn't feel like he cost me my dreams."

"Cost you your dreams? How would he be responsible for that?"

Mano stiffened. They'd already put a bit of a damper on the night. He didn't want to drive another nail in the coffin by talking about something that dark. "Let's not discuss it anymore tonight. I promise I'll tell you all about it another time."

"Okay."

The tempo of the music slowed and Paige surprised him by wrapping her arms around his neck. He pulled her close and they swayed together on the dance floor. Through the thin fabric of her dress, he could feel every inch of Paige pressing against him.

Suddenly, he wasn't interested in talking anymore. Or even dancing. He couldn't wait for the ship to return to the marina so he could slip off this dress and make love to Paige.

As they exited the elevator at their floor, Mano reached out and captured Paige around her waist. She allowed herself to press against him, relishing in the feeling of being in the arms of a man so strong and masculine. Walking with him this afternoon was nothing compared to how he made her feel now. He insisted that she was beautiful, and she almost believed it when he held her like this. Being as commanding of presence as he was, it was hard not to agree with anything he said. She couldn't understand how anyone could see him as handicapped. He simply couldn't see.

Everything else about him was amazing. He made *her* feel amazing and desirable. Just the touch of his hand against the bare small of her back tonight had sent a sizzle of need through her whole body. She could still feel the heat of his touch lingering there, as though his handprint had seared into her skin, branding her as his property.

She'd never imagined that she could capture the attention of a man like Mano, and yet here she was outside her hotel room, on the verge of asking him in. This wasn't like Paige at all. She'd never been one to indulge in casual sex, mostly because it was rarely offered. But something about the beauty of Mano and Hawaii mixed with pregnancy hormones made her feel braver than usual.

"Thank you for playing hooky with me today," she said instead of asking him in.

Mano tipped his head toward her face, although his gaze settled near her lips. "You're very welcome. I'll play hooky with you anytime you like, Paige."

"What about tomorrow?" she asked.

"Tomorrow?" Mano's voice was low and gruff. "Tomorrow is hours away. Right now I'm more concerned about tonight."

"Tonight?" Paige shifted just enough in his arms that she could feel the firm heat of Mano's erection pressing into her stomach. He wasn't just paying her lip service. He truly did want her, and he left no question of it. She wanted him, too, but in the heat of the moment, she felt a flutter of panic. This was really going to happen. She just had to say the word. Was she ready to take the leap?

Mano's hand reached up to caress her cheek. He stroked her skin and let the pad of his thumb brush across her bottom lip. His mouth followed, pressing his lips insistently to hers. She realized quickly that the answer was a definitive yes. She couldn't deny him. Not when he kissed her like this and held her as though he couldn't get enough of her.

Paige wasn't used to that kind of adoration. Wyatt's kisses had been nice enough, but they lacked a certain spark. Mano clearly enjoyed every second, and so did she. When her lips parted and his tongue glided across hers, he groaned. The low, primal sound made her insides pulse with a need she'd rarely felt before.

At last, reluctantly, she pulled away and tried to steady herself in his arms. The warmth of his skin and his masculine scent made her head swim with desire. Thoughts of tomorrow had faded away and all that mattered was here and now. She'd known they were spiraling toward this moment since they'd kissed on the balcony last night and he'd chased after her. She wanted him. She just had to be brave enough to ask for what she needed. "I would invite you into my room, but I don't know if you'd prefer us to go to your own suite. For Hōkū's sake."

Mano smiled at her. "That's an excellent idea. And very thoughtful." He pulled away, but not before taking her hand in his. "My suite, then?"

Before she could start to panic, they moved across the hall to his doorway and the reality of it all began to sink in. Inside, he cut Hōkū loose and went into the kitchen. "Can I get you something to drink? I have a couple kinds of beer, a bottle of Moscato, some pineapple juice and sparkling water."

"The water would be great," she said. His offer of alcohol was one she'd had to turn down repeatedly.

It was a reminder that she wasn't being as forthright with Mano as she should be. She couldn't put this off any longer. She'd told herself that if things got serious, she would tell him about the baby. Well, things were on the verge of seriousness. If it put a damper on their evening together, or ended this vacation romance altogether, so be it.

"Shall we drink on the patio?" he asked.

"Sure." She waited for him to open the bottle for her and a beer for himself. He handed hers over and they walked together to the sliding doors of the patio. They were both seated in the plush lounge chairs and gazing out at the dark sea before she worked up the nerve to say what she needed to say.

"Mano, before this goes any further, I need to tell you something."

He picked up his beer and took a sip. "Tell me anything, *pulelehua.*"

Paige hesitated for a moment. Did she really need to tell him about the baby? Their short vacation fling would long be a distant memory when her child was born, but somehow it didn't feel right to keep it from him.

"I'm leaving in less than a week, so it really doesn't matter, but I feel like I should tell you. I don't like keeping secrets, especially one that could be a potential turnoff for you."

Mano turned to her, a frown furrowing his brow. He sought out her hand and held it in his. "What is it? You're not married are you?" he asked with a joking grin.

"No," she said with a chuckle and a shake of her head. "But I am pregnant."

"Pregnant?" Mano's jaw fell slack with shock. She could tell it was the last thing he was expecting to hear.

"I know," Paige said, avoiding his gaze in favor of watching the waves below. "When I told you that my life was a little complicated right now, that's what I meant."

Mano put his hand over his heart. "You'll have to forgive me. It's the first time a woman has ever said those words to me. I had a moment of panic even though I know it couldn't be mine."

"I understand. It's not the kind of thing you'd expect me to say."

"When we touched, you didn't feel pregnant."

Paige remembered the surge of panic she'd felt the night before when he'd touched her stomach. "I'm only thirteen weeks along. I should start showing soon."

At last, Mano exhaled and took another big sip of his beer. "This explains a lot, actually. I couldn't fathom how someone could come all the way to Hawaii and not at least try a mai tai. I was wondering if you were a recovering alcoholic. This, however, is a very good reason."

"It is. I'd love to have a mai tai, honestly. With

the way my life is going, I could use a stiff drink."
Or a dozen.

"That doesn't sound good. Are there problems
with the baby's father?" he asked. "There must be
if you're here with me."

"You could say that. Long story short, you don't
need to worry about him. What happens between us
won't be some kind of torrid affair. He's out of the
picture. Permanently." Paige struggled to keep the
sound of tears out of her voice as she told the truth
about Wyatt, but the look of concern on Mano's face
was enough for her to know she'd failed.

"Does he know about the baby?"

Paige wished he hadn't asked that question. She'd
wrestled with that since she found out. She didn't
know how to tell him, or if Wyatt would even care.
He was with Piper now. The kind of man who would
dump one sister for the other was not likely to be
candidate for father of the year. She would tell him.
Maybe when she got back from Hawaii. But she
didn't expect the conversation to go well.

"Not yet," she admitted. "Like I said, it's complicated. I'm not going to bore you with my sob
story, but no matter what, I'm not going back to
him. That's the important part. I just wanted to tell
you the truth so you knew I wasn't trying to pull a
fast one on you and play it off as yours or something
else foolish. But at the same time, I hope it really

doesn't change things for us." She held her breath, waiting for his response.

"I beg to differ," Mano argued. "It does change things. For example, I'm certainly not going to send you parasailing or windsurfing now that I know you're pregnant."

Paige laughed at his protective response, relieved that he was joking about the whole thing instead of escorting her out of his suite. "I'm not fragile, I'm just pregnant."

"You're housing a life inside you, *pulelehua*. Enjoy yourself, but there's no need to be reckless."

Paige let out the breath she'd been holding, although her muscles were still tense. He seemed to take the news well, but she couldn't be sure. Would he handle her with kid gloves now? Send her back to her suite for a good night's rest without the sound bedding she'd hoped for? She didn't want to know, so she changed the subject by asking the question that had been bothering her for days.

"You keep calling me that Hawaiian word— *pule*something. What does it mean?"

*"Pulelehua,"* he repeated the complicated sounding word as though it simply rolled off his tongue. "It means 'butterfly.'"

Butterfly? Paige gasped aloud. Was this guy for real? He was like something out of a novel—the dashing romantic hero who says the right things and knows just how to touch a woman to make her melt with desire. She could feel the heat inside of her building and he hadn't even touched her yet. He was the kind of guy a girl like her would never have outside the pages of a book. And yet here he was with her, moments from the bedroom.

"That's sweet of you," she said, "but I feel more like a caterpillar most days."

Mano stood and reached for her hand. When she offered it, he pulled up her up and wrapped his arms around her waist. Paige relished the way her body fit so snugly against his. The press of her small and sensitive breasts against his chest created a sensation that made it almost hard to breathe, yet she wouldn't pull away. She couldn't. Her knees were so soft with desire that she'd melt to the floor if he let her go.

"You are no caterpillar, Paige, although sometimes I think you're still hiding in your cocoon, afraid to come out and spread your wings. You have challenges ahead of you, but I don't want you to think about them while you're here. This is your vacation getaway, and our fling is just the thing you need to get your mind off things. I don't want you to be afraid with me. I don't want you holding back. Especially not tonight."

She was holding back, but she had good reason not to leap into his arms and kiss him senseless. What if he wasn't there to catch her? "How can I not be afraid? You're like a dream I'm going to wake up from any moment now. I don't know why you chose me, but I'm on eggshells waiting for you to change your mind."

"I'm a very decisive man. I'm not the kind to change my mind. Especially not when I want you as badly as I do. So it's a very simple thing. Do you want me, *pulelehua*?"

Paige couldn't help the rush of air that purged from her lungs at the question. She didn't answer right away, instead reaching up to pull off his glasses. He didn't stop her, letting Paige gaze into his beautiful brown eyes, thankful she could see all of him. "I absolutely do. I'm scared to death, but I've never wanted a man more in my whole life."

Mano smiled and brushed the back of his hand across her cheek. His knuckles grazed her skin, leaving a trail of fire in their wake. "Good. Let's go back inside."

# Six

Mano led Paige down the length of his balcony to the second set of doors that opened into his master suite. He circled behind her and drew her back until her bare shoulder blades pressed into his chest. He let his palms run up her arms from her wrists to her shoulders, stopping at her neck when he found the tie of her dress. Her hair was up tonight, out of his way, so he had full access to the bare skin he'd hungered over on the yacht.

His fingers pulled gently at the fabric as he leaned in to leave a trail of kisses on the side of her neck and along her shoulders. When the knot finally came undone, he let go to see how far the fabric pooled. He felt down her sides, finding her bare waist, then hips, then thighs. The dress had simply slipped all the way to the floor.

"Thank you," he murmured into the sensitive hollow under her ear.

"Thank you for what?" she asked, her voice near breathless.

"Thank you for wearing a dress that was easy for me to take off. I don't have the patience to fuss with a lot of buttons and fasteners tonight. I was afraid I might have to tear the dress and buy you a new one."

Paige gasped, but he wasn't certain if it was the words or his hands reaching around her to cup her breasts. They were small, but firm, with nipples that hardened instantly to his touch. He massaged them gently, squeezing the tips until he could feel Paige shiver against him. She arched her back and pressed her hips into his raging desire, making him groan aloud against her neck.

"Oh, Paige," he whispered as he held one breast and let his other hand travel down her stomach. He detected the faintest roundness to her belly that ended just as he reached the lacy trim of her panties. His fingers dipped below the fabric and gently stroked between her thighs.

Paige writhed in his arms, her body wracked with the sensations of his touch. Encouraged, he stroked harder, teasing her in slow circles until she was panting and desperately clinging to the fabric of his suit coat. He hadn't intended to take this so far before they'd even reached the bed—he was still fully clothed, after all—but he couldn't bear to tease her. He wasn't about to let go of her until she was screaming his name.

Mano stroked at her moist flesh. Paige's knees buckled beneath her and she leaned back against him for support, which he gladly provided. It gave him an even better angle to her body. He took immediate advantage of it, letting a finger slip inside of her. She was so tight, he could feel her muscles clamp down around him as she whimpered with need.

"Mano…" she said in a pleading voice. He could feel the rest of her body tense and her heart race beneath his other hand as she came closer to her release.

"Yes, *pulelehua*," he encouraged in a low growl. "Fly for me, butterfly."

With one hard stroke, Paige came apart in his arms. She shuddered and cried out, her hips bucking against his hand as he held her tight to keep her from falling to the ground.

Mano waited until her breathing slowed and her body stilled. "Let's get you to bed."

"I won't argue with you on that," she murmured.

When Paige was stable on her feet, she took Mano's hand and let him lead her to the bed. She collapsed just at the edge, then moved quickly to re-

move his shirt. She wanted to see and touch him—
every inch of him. He didn't stop her. Instead, he
helped her by slipping out of his suit coat and tossing it into his corner chair.

Paige opened his shirt, tugging it out of his pants
so it could slip it off over his shoulders. That was
when she paused and took a moment to appreciate
the beauty of his body. His chest was solid muscle
and just as tan as the rest of him. The few scars she'd
glimpsed early that morning turned out to be more
numerous than she'd expected. They were old and
faded, standing out only because they were lighter
than his unblemished skin. It looked almost like the
chest of one of her soldiers that had taken shrapnel
from an explosion.

She let her fingertips trace every ridge of muscle,
tickling her way across his smooth chest and down
his stomach to stroke over his six-pack abs. His skin
was as soft and smooth as she wished her own could
be. "I have to admit I'm a little jealous," she said.

Mano chuckled. "Of what?" he asked.

"You have the smoothest, softest skin. Almost
no body hair at all. It's not fair, really."

"That's funny. I've always wanted some manly
chest hair. Genetically, it's just not common for my
people. My father was a white man stationed here
in the military, but even then, no luck. My Polynesian genes, along with my heritage, won out in
the e-end."

It seemed harder for Mano to get the words out as Paige continued to touch him. Her palms ran over his arms and shoulders, down his chest and finally to his belt. She was ready for the rest of him. Her belly burned for what would come next. The clink of the metal buckle gave way to the sound of his zipper drifting down. Impatiently, she slipped her hand inside, palming his massive erection and making a shudder run through his whole body.

"Paige," he groaned, but she didn't stop. It was her turn to play.

One hand stroked him while the other slipped off his pants and briefs. He stepped out of them, tossing them to the chair, as well. She figured that leaving clothing on the floor was like littering his space with land mines he would trip on later. She would be conscious to keep her own things out of his path.

Now Mano was naked, standing before her like an ancient Polynesian god. Not even the scars could detract from the carved beauty and masculinity of his body. Everything about him was large and strong. As her eyes took in his desire for her, she swallowed hard. She went to reach for him and then she remembered an important step. "Before we go any further," Paige said. "Do you have condoms somewhere?"

Mano nodded and pointed to the bed stand. "There should be a new box in there."

Paige opened up the drawer and pulled out the

largest box of condoms she'd ever seen outside a bulk warehouse. She couldn't contain her nervous laughter. "A twenty-count box?"

He grinned and shrugged. "I was feeling hopeful yesterday after our kiss," he said. "I bought them at the gift shop last night. It might seem like a lot, but we are spending the week together, you know. I think a solid goal would be to use every single one before you leave."

Paige had a hard time believing they were having sex at all, much less twenty times, but she would be happy to aim high. "Ambitious. I like that."

Mano held still as Paige opened a condom and slowly rolled it down his length. He bit at his bottom lip as she took her time and stroked every last air pocket out.

"You're pretty good at putting those on for a pregnant lady."

At that, Paige laughed aloud. "Touché." She reached out and stroked his undercarriage to punish him in the best way possible.

Mano hissed through gritted teeth and pulled away from her touch. He moved past her to the bed and threw back the comforter. Taking Paige by the wrist, he pulled her onto the bed beside him. The lengths of their whole bodies were touching, skin to skin at last, with his need for her insistently pressing against her belly.

His hands went back to her body, seeking out her

sensitive center. He stroked and teased at her again until she was more than ready for him. He rolled her onto her back and she parted her thighs so he could settle there. Without hesitation, he surged forward and filled her.

Paige gasped as the pleasure-pain of it shot through her. Once the feeling faded, she lifted her hips to take all of him in, wrapping her legs around his hips to pull him in deeper. It was a delicious sensation, one unlike any feeling she'd experienced before. Judging by his tightly clenched jaw and tensed muscles, Mano was enjoying the position, too. She wanted to immediately give in to it and relieve the tension he built inside of her. They had nineteen condoms left, after all, but she knew he wasn't about to let this end so soon.

He started by stroking long, slow and deep inside of her. Propping himself up on one arm, he cupped her breast with his free hand. Since her pregnancy, they had become extremely sensitive. The nipple pebbled at his touch, growing hard against his caress and making her moan with pleasure.

"What color are your nipples, Paige?" he asked.

Paige was startled from the sensation by his bold question. "Um…" She didn't know what to say.

"If I could see them, I wouldn't have to ask. Tell me, please."

That was true. She needed to open up so she

could share every aspect of this moment with him. "Dark pink. Almost a dusky rose, I guess."

Mano nodded slowly, biting his lower lip with his eyes closed as though he were picturing them in his mind. Bending down, he took one into his mouth. His tongue flickered over it, making Paige squirm beneath him. The moist heat of his mouth on her skin coaxed pleasure that made her core tighten and pulse around him.

He hesitated only for a moment and then he redoubled his efforts to pleasure her. His hips moved in a more circular motion, making his pelvis grind against her sensitive nub. He timed the strokes with the hard suction of her breast until Paige was a gasping, writhing, moaning mess beneath him. She'd never allowed herself to unravel like this before, but she could do it with him and not feel self-conscious about it.

"Are you close, *pulelehua*?"

"Oh yes," she whimpered. "So close."

"What do you want me to do?" he asked.

"Love me harder," she demanded softly. "Fill me and don't be gentle."

Mano made a growling sound deep in his throat before dropping onto his elbows on each side of her. He buried one hand in her hair and the other gripped her shoulder tight. He thrust hard once, making Paige cry out loud. He followed it with two more hard strokes, then he seemed to let go of whatever restraint he had left. He pumped hard and fast into her body, holding tight as his hips pounded into hers.

Paige's cries escalated from soft gasps and whimpers to loud screams as he unleashed his passion on her. "Yes! Yes!" she shouted, loving every minute of it. She loved the feel of his skin, slick with sweat against her own. Her cries echoed in her own ears, their scent growing stronger the harder he loved her. Her every sense was overloaded, pushing her closer to the edge as he climbed there himself.

Then it hit her. Her release was punctuated with a sharp cry of pleasure she couldn't hold in. He continued to thrust into her as her internal muscles tightened and fluttered around him. Before her last gasps faded, he finally gave in to it and poured into her with a loud groan of satisfaction.

Paige welcomed him into her arms as he collapsed, spent, against her. Finally rolling to her side, Mano sank into the pillows. With one hand curled over her left breast, they fell asleep together with her heartbeat serving as the soothing rhythm that lured them to sleep.

Paige woke up in the night practically starving. She never woke up to eat in the middle of the night, and she'd had plenty to eat at dinner. The pregnancy books she'd read said that once she reached her second trimester, the cravings would begin in earnest, and that must be what was behind it. Why did this have to happen when she was naked and in the bed of a sexy hotelier? He probably didn't have much food in that kitchen. Of course, she didn't have any in her suite, either.

As quietly as she could, Paige peeled back the covers and slipped from bed. With her only option being her red gown, she considered just going hunting for food in the nude. No one would see her but Hōkū, anyway. But propriety got the best of her and she found Mano's robe hanging in the bathroom like the one in her own suite. She wrapped herself up in it and padded barefoot through the bedroom into the living room area.

Hōkū was asleep on his pillow, but his head popped up when he saw her. He got up and followed her lazily into the kitchen. He sat by her side as she opened the refrigerator door and frowned. Beer, water, juice and fancy dog food.

"That's no help," she said to the dog, then turned to check cabinets for pantry goods. She found dog biscuits, some saltines and a box of Pop Tarts. Paige never thought of Mano as a Pop Tart guy, but she supposed everyone had their weaknesses. Unfortunately, that was not what she wanted. She got a dog biscuit out anyway and gave it to Hōkū. He happily wagged his tail and lay down on the floor to eat his treat.

"We found something for you, but nothing for

me. My dorm room in college had more food than this and I was broke," she muttered.

"That's because your dorm room didn't have room service."

Startled, Paige spun on her heels to see Mano standing in the doorway to the kitchen. He had tugged on a pair of boxer briefs, but otherwise, he was still gloriously bare. Her heart was beating too quickly to appreciate it, though. "Lord," she swore. "You scared the hell out of me."

"Sorry. Usually people are sneaking up on me, not the other way around."

She supposed that was true. "I was trying not to wake you up. Sorry."

"No worries," he said, leaning against the wall. "I don't sleep well. To me, it's dark all the time, so my body never knows when it's time to rest and when it's time to wake up. What did you need?"

Paige sighed and opened the refrigerator door again as though things would change. "I'm hungry. I shouldn't be, it's two in the morning, but the baby has other ideas."

"Tell me what you want and I'll have it brought up."

"It's two in the morning," Paige repeated. "Doesn't the kitchen close?"

"Not entirely. There's twenty-four-hour service for special guests, including the two penthouse suites. So, lucky you, you can have whatever you'd like."

That was tempting. Or it would be if she could pin down what she was after. The baby wasn't quite specific enough. "Would you eat some of it?"

"Sure." He shrugged. Mano picked up his phone and dialed it. "This is Mr. Bishop," he said after a moment. "Yes, I'd like to place an order to be brought up. One second." He stopped and handed the phone to her. "Order anything and everything you'd like."

Paige felt like she was living out the *Pretty Woman* breakfast scene. Her brain wanted everything on the menu, but she held it in. "Hello?" she said.

"Yes, ma'am? What can we get for you?"

"I don't know. I don't have a room service menu."

"That's fine. We can make whatever you'd like."

Paige could get used to this. "Well, how about a cheese and fruit plate with some crackers?"

"Yes, ma'am. Anything else?"

"A Sprite. And…" Her hungry brain started to spin. "A chocolate milkshake. That's all."

"Very well, ma'am. It will be up shortly."

When she hung up the phone, Mano was smiling at her. "What?" she asked.

"Nothing." He took a few steps toward her and Paige closed the gap to walk into his arms. "You're just adorable."

"Adorable?" she repeated. "I'll take it, but it's not really what I was going for."

Mano laughed. "Well, earlier, you were a wild sex kitten, if that makes you feel better. Right now, you and your food cravings are cute."

Paige leaned in to rest her head against his chest. "They're cute now. They won't be cute when I'm huge and home alone and there's no room service to bring me what I want. Then it will just be sad."

Mano's expression fell and his lips twisted in thought. "Are you sure the father won't be there for you?"

Paige's mind drifted to the disturbing image of her sister in Wyatt's arms. It was almost as awkward as talking about the baby's father with her new lover. "Yes, I'm pretty sure. I'm also sure I don't *want* him to be there for me. He was a bad choice. My biological and emotional urges overrode my common sense. At the very least, I hope the baby will take after him physically. The father is very handsome, if nothing else. I can raise the baby to be more kind and thoughtful than he was. That will be easier without his influence."

Mano's furrowed brow didn't disappear no matter how she tried to dismiss the father. "I don't like the idea of you doing this alone."

Paige nearly snorted. Join the club! "Yes, well, things are what they are. The baby and I will be fine on our own."

"What...what if you moved here?"

Paige froze. What the hell did he mean by that?

The expression on his face was perfectly serious, but that couldn't be the case. "Moved here? I can barely afford a place in San Diego. I certainly can't afford anything on Oahu."

"You wouldn't have to," he insisted. "I could get you a place. Make sure that you had everything you needed for you and the baby. You could work or not, whatever you wanted. Wouldn't that make things easier for you?"

"Sure, but what do you get in return? Am I your on-call piece on the side whenever you're feeling lonely?"

"What?" Mano looked horrified. "No! I'm just being nice. I'm not buying your affections like a common prostitute. There are no strings to this, even if we never slept together again. I asked for a week with you and that's all I'd require."

No matter how many words came out of his mouth, Paige didn't understand what he was talking about. Why would a man offer to support a woman and another man's baby with nothing in return? "Why would you do that? You hardly know me."

"I know enough about you. I've got more money than I could ever spend, and it sounds like you are in a rough spot. Let me help you out."

Paige's eyes grew wide. "Oh no," she said dismissively. "I'm not going to be a charity case. Thanks, though."

"I can't win with you. Either I get something out

of this and you feel cheap or I don't and you feel like I'm pitying you. I wish you wouldn't look at it that way." Mano approached her and put his hands on her arms. "Let me do this for you. I want to. And you could use the help if you'd just admit it. At least think about it."

The doorbell to the suite rang and Paige was grateful for the interruption. "I'll get it," she said, pulling away from his touch.

Paige opened the door and room service came in with a cart. "Where would you like it?" the man asked.

She motioned over to the dining room table. "That's fine."

She was handed the room service receipt, but the total was blank. The perks of owning the hotel, she supposed. She filled out the tip generously and handed it back. The man quickly disappeared, leaving her alone with a delectable chocolate milkshake and an uncomfortable conversation.

Paige opted to ignore their previous discussion and focused on her food instead. Under the lid was a beautifully arranged platter with at least five or six types of cheeses, an assortment of crackers, strawberries, grapes, pineapple and apple slices. It was just what she'd been wanting.

"Would you like to eat on the balcony?" Mano asked.

"Actually, if it's okay, I'd be happy just to take it to bed. I eat in bed a lot at home."

"Not a problem."

Paige gathered up her tray and carried it into the bedroom. She placed it on the foot of the bed, moving her drink and her milkshake to the nightstand. She stacked the pillows high behind her and curled up in the blankets. Mano joined her, snuggling to her side and thankfully not bringing up their earlier discussion.

They chatted about harmless things and nibbled on the food. Paige fed Mano grapes and even shared her milkshake with him. It was an easy, fun moment together in the middle of the night. She hadn't had many experiences where sex was followed by conversation and cuddling. It was nice. Being with Mano was nice.

But when the food was gone and they'd opted to go back to sleep, Paige couldn't turn her brain off. Thoughts swirled through her mind faster than she could process them. She lay there amongst the pillows with Mano snoring softly next to her. It felt amazing to be here beside him. Wonderful. She enjoyed spending time with him more than she ever expected to.

And maybe that was the problem she had with his offer. He didn't ask her to stay because he loved her. They'd only been together a few days, so she'd wonder if he was insane if he did. He didn't ask her to move here because he wanted to be with her for more than just a week. That might even be different enough for her to consider it. Instead, he was just trying to solve her problems and help her take care of her baby, which was noble, but it wasn't what she wanted from him.

Raising her baby alone would be hard. There would be long hours with day care or a sitter when she worked nights. There would be miserable sleepless days where they would both be cranky and exhausted. But there would also be the two of them together like peanut butter and jelly.

Paige had wondered often if she would spend most of her life alone. She'd never been in a serious enough relationship to imagine herself getting married or having children. She feared she might become one of those lonely spinsters who talked to cats. She liked cats. But she didn't like the idea of going through her whole life on her own.

Wyatt was a first-rate jerk, but he had given her something she never expected to have. No matter what, she would have this baby and she wouldn't be alone. It wasn't the same as having a partner in life, but it was something. There would always be a little part of her out in the world that loved her unconditionally, gave her sweet kisses and remembered her birthday. She looked forward to handmade construction paper and crayon cards, and jewelry made of macaroni and glitter.

And maybe one day in the future, instead of cats, she would have grandchildren to love and dote on. She couldn't ask for anything better than that.

No, as generous as Mano's offer was, she couldn't accept it. Paige would do this on her own.

# Seven

"You work too much, Mano. I called you last night at nine thirty and it rolled over to voice mail."

"Aloha to you, too, *Kalani*," Mano responded to his brother's phone call. As much as he'd hated to leave Paige asleep in bed, he needed to get *some* work done today. He'd slipped downstairs early in the hopes he could perhaps take a half day. He liked playing hooky when Paige was involved, but he did still have a hotel to oversee. "What makes you think I didn't answer because I was working?"

"Is there another option for you?" Kal asked with a chuckle. "I mean, it's not like you were with a woman."

Mano grinned silently and waited for Kal to piece it together.

"You *were* with a woman? That's a welcome change."

"Shut up," Mano chastised. He didn't feel much like getting ragged on by his brother today, but he should've thought of that before he answered the phone. "It's not as though it's my first go out the gate. I've been with plenty of women."

"Oh sure. There was that belly dancer from Qatar, what, six months ago?"

"Five." It was just like his brother to keep track of his sex life just so he could rub it in his face.

"And the Australian opera singer? That was before Thanksgiving, I think."

He had him there. "Probably. You know how I am. Once or twice a year, if I'm lucky, I find a lady with whom I'm interested in spending a little time. It just so happens, I've found one to be with this week."

"What's this one? A Brazilian bikini model? You seem to be trying to cover every continent."

"You're one to talk, Kal. I can't help it I live in Hawaii and run a hotel. I'm surrounded by tourists. This time is no different. But no, she's not a bikini model. She's actually a nurse from San Diego."

"Interesting choice. So, what drew you to this one? It couldn't be the accent this time."

"Actually, no. It was her scent. And her total and complete awkwardness. It was charming."

"I have to say, I've never chosen a woman for being clumsy, but more power to you, man, if it gets you away from your desk for a while."

Mano smiled. Paige had certainly done that. "I took yesterday off to spend the day with her."

"Really?" He could hear the disbelief in Kal's voice. "I don't recall you doing that for Miss Qatar."

"That was because she was with a couple of friends that went out during the day. Paige is here alone."

"What kind of person comes to Hawaii alone?"

Mano sighed. He didn't really want to get into Paige's story with Kal. "The kind of person that could use a vacation and a knowledgeable tour guide."

"What good are you as a tour guide if you won't leave the property?"

"We left the property!" Mano snapped at his older brother. Kal always thought he knew everything. He was older and wiser, while Mano was just the baby. It had only gotten worse after their parents died. At that point, Kal decided he was the head of the family and needed to not only run the show but care for Mano as though he were still a child. Never mind he was nearly eighteen at the time he lost his eyesight.

"Okay, okay," Kal said. "How long is the nurse from San Diego in town?"

"Until Friday afternoon."

"That's a shame. I'm going to just miss her."

"How's that?"

"I'm flying over on Sunday for Tūtū Ani's birthday. You didn't forget about her party, did you?"

Yes. "No," Mano insisted. "I wouldn't forget our grandmother's birthday. I just thought you'd be too busy to come."

"You're the workaholic, little brother, not me. Of course I'm coming. After a week with your friend, I expect you to be in a good mood when I arrive."

"Don't get your hopes up on that. You know those big family gatherings always make me tense."

"Your family should be where you feel the most at ease," Kal argued.

"Yes, well, I only feel at ease at the Mau Loa. So unless they're having the party here and neglected to tell me so I could book the ballroom, I won't be having much fun. But I'll go for Tūtū Ani's sake."

Honestly, it wasn't just the location that stressed Mano out. The large crowd of family, the well-meaning but pushy aunts treating him like an invalid, the kids running in front of him and unnerving Hōkū…it all added up to an afternoon he'd sooner do without. He hadn't really even enjoyed the gatherings when his parents were alive and he could see.

"You know they're having it at Aunt Kini's place. It's the only place we can bury the pig."

Thank goodness Paige was here. That's all Mano had to say about it. She would be a welcome distraction from the upcoming chaos. Hell, he'd completely forgotten about his grandmother's birthday celebration until Kal mentioned it. He'd be happy to lose his memory once again in Paige's arms.

"Did we get her a gift?" Mano asked. He couldn't remember.

Kal just sighed into the phone. "Yes. We went in together to get her the golden South Sea pearl necklace with the diamond clasp. You don't remember sending me a check for that? People usually remember paying that much for something."

Mano just shrugged. "We both have more money than we'll ever spend. I really don't pay attention to things like that."

"Well, at least pay attention to your phone. I'm going to text you when my plane leaves Maui. I need you to send the car to pick me up."

"Okay." Mano made a note of his brother's arrival and his grandmother's party in his calendar so he wouldn't forget again. "I'll see you Sunday. Don't take it personally if I don't answer the phone between now and then."

Kal barked an evil laugh into the phone. "I won't. I know you're getting busy. I mean, you're busy."

"Goodbye, dork."

Mano heard his brother laugh again into the phone as he ended the call. He loved Kal, but he certainly didn't mind that they lived on separate islands now. He was happy to have his space, from his brother and from the rest of the family. At the Mau Loa, he was in charge and confident of his every move. Although they knew he ran the family business without a hitch, his family was still prone to treating him as though he were newly blind and incapable of doing anything for himself.

They certainly wouldn't believe what he'd done over the last few days. His little adventures with Paige had been out of the norm for him. While it made him uneasy, it also was a shot of excitement into a life he'd crafted to be very predictable and dull.

Paige was anything but, and he liked that about her. It made him wish, for the first time, that she wasn't a tourist. Going into these short-term flings, Mano could always guarantee that he knew when the relationship would end. There was no reason to worry about an ugly breakup or a woman walking out on him, like Jenna had. Paige was the first woman who made him want more. He didn't know what more he wanted, but he wasn't looking forward to the end of the week.

It would come, though, so he needed to mentally prepare for that. She'd turned down his offer to stay on Oahu, flat. The offer had been part charity, part selfishness. He could help her, and he wanted to, especially if she might be in his life for a while longer. Her negative reaction stopped him cold. That meant that no matter how charming, sexy or wonderful Paige was, he couldn't let himself get wrapped up in this. It was just a fling. That's all he wanted. He just needed to keep reminding himself of that when he was around her.

Mano's phone chirped again, but this time it was a text. He pressed the button to have the phone read it aloud.

It was Paige. *"You snuck out on me! I thought we were spending today together."*

He laughed as the phone's voice read Paige's text aloud. He hit the button to dictate a response. "It's still early, *pulelehua*. We have plenty of time to be together yet, today." The phone repeated his words back to confirm the text before it sent his response.

It chimed again. *"Okay, but if we're going all the way to the North Shore and back today, we shouldn't get too late a start."*

Mano's brow raised curiously at her response. The North Shore? They hadn't even discussed that possibility. "Is that what we're doing today?"

*"Yes. We're getting garlic scampi shrimp and sticky rice from a food truck and eating it on the beach."*

Ah. She'd been reading some of the brochures he'd given her for sights around the island. "I hope you're driving," he replied and got a smiley face in return. "I'll reserve a car from the hotel fleet."

Mano got up to talk to the head of hotel transportation with a smile on his face. He knew exactly which car they needed to take out—the cherry red convertible roadster. The little BMW was one of the special touches he'd added to the hotel for exclusive guests to use to see the island. His teenage heart wished he could be the one to drive it—it was the car he'd dreamt of when he had turned sixteen—but he'd settle for riding shotgun. Being beside Paige was enough to make his heart race and his adrenaline rush through his veins.

They'd take this trip so she could experience more of his home, but he was far more interested in coming back to the hotel so he could have her again. Unless, of course, they could find a secluded enough spot on the North Shore...

This was potentially the messiest and best thing she'd ever eaten. An old white food truck in a patch of dirt off the highway had just served her a plate of shrimp so divinely garlicky and buttery, she had streams of butter and olive oil dripping down her forearms as she tried to eat. Mano had opted for the spicy shrimp, and she could already see beads of sweat forming on his forehead from the hot chilies. They'd taken their order to go and found a piece of rocky secluded shoreline a few miles away, where Paige spread a blanket out on a dry stretch of sand for them to have a picnic.

The sea was wilder here on the North Shore, less manicured and tourist friendly than Waikiki. The sand was decorated with chunks of black volcanic rock and large pieces of driftwood from trees that had fallen. The deeper water was a stormy blue, but the shallow tide pools just beyond them were perfectly clear. She was certain she would put her feet in them before they left. They called to her.

"This is a beautiful spot," she said, immediately feeling guilty that he couldn't see it. "It's such a nice day."

"I always liked it up here," Mano said as he sipped his drink. "When I was a teenager, some of the guys and I would come down here to pretend like we could really surf. I'm surprised none of us got killed. The waves out here are for professionals, but we wanted to show off for the girls."

"I can't believe you'd risk that just to impress a girl." That seemed crazy, but she'd seen boys do plenty of daredevil stunts to get a girl's attention.

"One girl in particular," Mano admitted. "We dated for two years. Jenna." He winced as he said her name, as though it pained him. "I was a fool for her. I would've done any stupid thing she asked to see her smile and beam at me with pride."

"What happened with Jenna?" She felt like she shouldn't pry, but at the same time, she wanted to know since he had brought it up.

"Like most things in my life, the accident happened."

Paige was afraid of that. "Will you tell me about it now, since you wouldn't last night?"

Mano sighed and set down his carton of food.

"Do you really want to ruin a beautiful day on the beach in Hawaii with my sob story?"

"Yes."

He shrugged and leaned forward to pick at his food with a fork. "My brother, Kal, was playing football at the University of Hawaii. My parents and I were driving to the stadium to see the game. On the way there, we came upon one of the little pop-up rainstorms we have around here. It wasn't a big deal, they disappear in minutes, but an oncoming SUV was going too fast through a curve. I was in the backseat, so I'm not entirely sure what happened, but the police seemed to think the SUV hit a pool of water and hydroplaned into us at full speed."

Paige held her breath as he told the story. She knew it wasn't going to end well, and yet she kept hoping she was wrong.

"They had to use heavy machinery to extract us from the car, but I don't remember anything about it. I woke up in the hospital a couple days later and started screaming because I couldn't see. They had to drug me and restrain my arms because I just went completely berserk. I didn't even care that my arm was broken. I accidentally hit a nurse with my cast and blackened her eye. I didn't know she was there, but in the moment, I just didn't care about anything but my sight and when it was coming back. It wasn't, of course."

Mano shook his head and frowned. "I was such a

mess that they didn't tell me my parents were dead for almost a week. I missed their funeral while I was in the hospital. Kal and my grandparents had to face all of that on their own."

"I'm sorry about your parents. I didn't know about that." Paige never dreamed the story would be worse than she imagined. He hadn't mentioned his parents very often, though, so she should've anticipated it.

"Yeah. The hardest part for me, I think, was that I never really got to mourn them. I just snapped my fingers and they were gone. Once I got out of the hospital, I was in and out of rehabilitation and training for my new disability. I had to learn braille and adapt every aspect of my life to being blind. Technology is better now, but even just a decade ago, there was a steep learning curve. There wasn't really time to think about losing them and what it meant for my life."

"What about the rest of your family?"

"My grandparents took over hotel operations again. They'd retired when they handed it over to my parents, but they knew Kal and I weren't ready for the responsibility. Kal dropped out of school for the rest of the semester and came home to take care of me. I think he felt guilty. He wouldn't leave my side for a minute."

"Why? Survivor's guilt?"

"Not quite. I think he decided none of it would've

happened if he hadn't wanted us to come to his game that night. It's ridiculous, really, but even though he won't say it, I think he believes it. His life has turned into a penance. He completely changed course and seemed to pick up my life where I left it off, so my dreams could still be fulfilled in some twisted way. The Maui hotel was my plan. He opened it for me, which isn't the same, but I appreciate it. When I was old enough, I took over the Oahu hotel since I was familiar and more comfortable with it. I converted one of the penthouses into my apartment so I didn't have to commute or worry about the world outside the Mau Loa. And here we are."

"And what about Jenna?"

For the first time since he started telling his story, Mano turned to face the sea. His jaw hardened. Hōkū seemed to sense the change in his mood and rested his head on Mano's thigh in support. Mano placed his hand on the dog and stroked absentmindedly. "We had big dreams, too. We were going to go to college together, get married and run the new resort as a team like my parents and grandparents had. At first, she was right there by my side, but I think she had a naïveté about the accident. Like if she hung on long enough, I'd get my vision back and we could continue on with our plans. When that didn't happen, she left."

"Really?" Paige's heart ached at the thought.

"Yes. She said that she was too young to throw

away her whole life taking care of me. And she was right. I don't blame her for going. I was enough of a burden on my family. I've no interest in being a rock that drags her—or any other woman—down."

Paige sat back on her heels and considered this confession. She'd seen the same thing with her soldiers. While they would die for their brothers, they refused to hold each other—or anyone else—back. She worried that some of them would've rather died on the battlefield than come home and be a strain on their family and friends. A lot of them pushed people away, not letting anyone close.

"So, is that why a handsome, rich hotel magnate is single and sitting on a beach with me instead of charming his beautiful wife and playing with their children?"

He shrugged. Mano didn't seem to want to get too introspective about the whole thing. "There's no sense wasting my time in real relationships. Spending this week with you, or another week with another woman every now and then, is all I need. I get the excitement, the passion, and it all ends before things can turn sour."

Mano had been right. As much as she wanted to know about his past, the story had certainly taken their afternoon on a darker turn. The oily shrimp started to churn in her stomach. She knew their time together would be short and without strings, but somehow knowing that he deliberately kept women, including her, at arm's length made her sad. She wasn't entertaining any romantic delusions about the two of them, but she still found herself caring more for Mano than she intended to. He did care about her and the baby, too, in his own way. He wouldn't have offered to help her if he didn't. He wouldn't be trying so hard to make her feel better about herself if he didn't worry at least a little about her. But it was different. She wanted him to be happy and she just didn't see that in him, despite his protestations.

Instead of dwelling on it, she tried to make light of his confession. "So you just want me because I'll be gone in a few days," she teased, thankful that he couldn't see the glimmer of hurt in her eyes. "Tell the truth."

He instantly brightened, happy to put all that aside. "You bet. I want you more the shorter our time together gets." Mano leaned toward her and beckoned her to kiss him. She complied, pressing her lips against his. She let herself give in to the kiss. That was what this week was about anyway. Enjoyment. Pleasure. Not dwelling in the past or worrying about the future. She just found it hard to turn those parts of her brain off.

When Mano's hand found her breast and cupped it through her tank top, she finally succeeded in focusing on the here and now. She moaned softly against his lips as his thumb stroked her nipples though the thin cotton. She hadn't worn a bra today—one of the perks of being a thin, nearly flat-chested woman. That meant there was very little separating the two of them.

She lay back on the blanket and let Mano roll onto his side next to her. He tugged gently at the neckline of her top, exposing her breast so he could capture it with his mouth. Paige buried her fingers in the long, dark waves of his hair and pulled him closer to her.

Paige loved getting lost in the feel of being with Mano. His mouth and hands and body on her were like nothing else in her life before now. There was no hesitation in his touch. Mano seemed convinced that she was beautiful and, for now, she'd let him believe that. Maybe they'd make it through the week before he learned the truth.

Eventually, someone would tell him. Staff at the hotel, maybe? Perhaps he'd overhear someone ask aloud why a man like him was with a woman like her. That would have to make him wonder. But until then, she would try to enjoy it.

There was a freedom in being with a man who couldn't see her. It took a while for her to adjust to the idea of not feeling self-conscious all the time, but once she got used to it, she really loved it. Some might find it a cruel irony that an unattractive woman would end up with a blind man, but to her, it was such a relief. At least until he realized that he was the one getting the short end of the stick.

She tried not to let those thoughts ruin the moment and focused instead on his touch. Mano's hand slipped beneath her shorts and sought out her center. He started stroking her, gently at first, then harder. Her breath caught in her throat as the sensations starting exploding inside of her. Within a minute she was close to coming undone. She couldn't believe how quickly he could manipulate her body into doing whatever he wanted it to do.

Paige looked around in a panic as she got closer… Anyone could see them together like this. Mano didn't seem to care, of course, but he wouldn't know if someone was watching.

"Someone is going to see us," she panted.

Mano raised his head from her breast. "I doubt it."

"What if they hear us?"

Mano chuckled and nuzzled her neck, never slowing his sensual exploration of her body. "Are you planning to be loud?"

"I may not have a choice in the matter."

"Good."

Mano rubbed harder, dipping his finger inside of her and stroking her from the inside, as well. The combination was explosive, sending her over the edge without a care if someone were watching them or not. He kissed her just as she reached the pinnacle, smothering her cries with his mouth until she finally stilled beside him.

Just as she returned to reality, a sound caught Paige's attention. She pulled Mano's hand away and quickly adjusted her shirt as she sat up on the blanket. Behind them, another car had pulled up beside theirs. A whole family climbed out, talking and laughing all at once. She watched the father haul out chairs and a cooler and knew that their private oasis was gone. They'd just barely made it.

"I think we'll have to finish what we started back at the hotel," she said.

"It's probably for the best," Mano agreed as he sat up and dusted the sand off his legs. "A little make-out session is one thing, but any more serious action and sand gets *everywhere*. It's very unpleasant."

Paige smiled and leaned in to give him a kiss. "So you're promising me some serious action when we get back to the hotel?"

Mano pulled her close and deepened the kiss. "You better believe it."

# Eight

Paige pried one eye open in the early morning light. She could see Mano slipping into his suit coat and frowned. "Where are you going?" she asked with a pout.

"Work. Just for a little while," he said sitting down on the edge of the bed. He leaned in and she met him halfway for a goodbye kiss. "A couple of hours. I'll meet you for lunch. What are you going to do this morning while I'm gone?"

Paige considered her options. It was already Thursday and there was so much of the resort she hadn't seen. She really should take the opportunity to explore something other than Mano's bed. "I thought I might walk through the shops and browse at some point. I also thought about going to the pool. I haven't done that yet."

"That would be nice. Go swimming first. Most of the shops don't open until ten. By the time you finish and shower, they'll be open."

Paige twisted her lips in thought. "That's a good idea. I doubt I'll buy anything, though. The shops I've seen are all very high end. I'm not coming back upstairs with a Louis Vuitton bag."

Mano reached out and stroked her cheek with the back of his hand. Paige leaned in to his touch, wishing more and more than he didn't insist on going to work so soon. "If you want one, you should get one. Have them charge it to me. Anything you want, just tell them."

Paige laughed aloud, eliciting a frown from Mano. "What's funny?" he asked.

"You. Since I arrived in Hawaii, it's like I live in an alternate dimension. Penthouse suites, room service, you offering to buy me anything I want… it's all kind of ridiculous. Really. You should see my apartment. You'd be horrified."

Mano sighed and shook his head. "Then consider your time here a little pampering. I mean it—buy something today. I'll check my charges, and if there isn't anything on there, I'll be very disappointed."

"Okay," she finally agreed. Paige fully intended

to buy a pack of gum at the sundries store just to say she bought something.

He leaned in and kissed her again before whistling for Hōkū. "I'll meet you for lunch at about noon, okay? I'll text you to see where you are."

Paige nodded and watched him walk away. Rolling onto her back, she stretched leisurely across the king-size mattress and stared up at the ceiling. A few hours by the pool might be just what she needed. It was early enough that she might not have to fight for a lounge chair.

She pulled her hair up into a knot on the top of her head and slipped into the bikini she bought for the trip. It was a bright blue and purple design with a halter top and boy shorts for the bottoms. The cut gave her the illusion of curves where she had none.

Before she pulled on her cover-up, she decided to slather on some sunblock so it could soak in. As her hands slid across her belly, she realized she was finally starting to show. The change was subtle, just the slightest curve, but it was enough for her to notice on her slight frame. She turned sideways to look at herself in the mirror and admire her burgeoning baby bump.

At the moment it just looked like a big lunch, but she would be growing at a faster pace from here on out. The baby would be doubling in size every few weeks. It was easy to ignore her situation while her belly was flat, but soon her pregnancy would be common knowledge to anyone who saw her.

With a sigh, Paige slipped the royal blue cover-up over her suit and gathered things to take to the pool with her. She tossed the sunblock, her phone, earbuds and a book in the wicker shoulder bag she bought on the beach and headed downstairs.

It was hard to believe she hadn't made it to the pool yet. Paige had admired it every time she walked past but hadn't dipped her toe in even once. It was beautiful, beckoning to her. The pool looked like a natural, sprawling lagoon surrounded by large stone boulders and green, leafy plants, as though it were nestled in a tropical rain forest. Hidden among the boulders was a pair of slides and a couple waterfalls.

Paige found a lounge chair in a corner with a little bit of shade. The touch of sunburn she'd gotten on their first day out had started to fade, and she didn't want to make it worse. She laid out one of the fluffy pool towels and self-consciously glanced around to see if anyone was looking before she slipped out of her cover-up. The coast was clear, so she whipped it up over her head and settled down into the chair.

One of the poolside servers approached her after a few minutes. "May I bring you anything?" he asked.

She wanted coffee, but that wasn't on her menu. "Pineapple juice and seltzer water would be great. Thank you." The fresh juice and bubbles would be a nice change. Decadent, but not too much for the early morning.

The waiter disappeared and Paige relaxed back into her chair. As the sun warmed her skin, she closed her eyes and tried to enjoy it all. Her time in Hawaii had been filled with activity, both in and out of Mano's bed, so she hadn't gotten much R&R time. This was her chance. All that was missing was music. She pulled her phone and her earbuds out of her bag and cued up her favorite playlist.

Just before she hit Play, she noticed two women sit down in the lounge chairs nearby. She didn't pay much attention to them, though; she wasn't in the mood to chat. But as the first song ended with a short period of silence before the next song, she caught a bit of the conversation beside her.

"That's the woman I was telling you about," the blonde said in a harsh whisper that was anything but quiet.

"Her? *Really?*" Her friend, a brunette, sounded aghast.

Paige knew she could turn up the music and drown out their voices, but instead she hit Pause so she could listen without their knowledge. She was a masochist that way.

"It's unbelievable, right? I saw the two of them together the other night. Even when they were all dressed up, she wasn't anything to look at. I don't know what he sees in her. Oh wait." The blonde laughed. "He doesn't see anything."

The two women laughed, making Paige clench her teeth. She was used to people having opinions about her, but she didn't like hearing them mock Mano. That was uncalled for.

"She's got her headphones on, right?" the brunette asked.

"Yes, she can't hear us. But even if she could… she knows as well as we do that they're an aesthetic mismatch. There's no way a rich hunk like that would be with a woman like her if he wasn't blind."

Paige struggled not to react and hoped her sunglasses hid away the emotions that slipped out anyway. She never should've listened to their conversation. She had known what she was in for and now she'd let it ruin a perfectly good morning by the pool. The most painful part of the whole discussion was the fact that the woman was right. Paige did know they were an odd match, and she agreed with them. She'd had the same thoughts a dozen times since Mano kissed her. Would he feel the same if he could see her? She worried the answer was no, but he was the only one who disagreed.

"Someone sounds jealous," the brunette taunted her friend.

"I'm not jealous!" the other woman snapped. "I just think that if the guy could stand the two of us side by side and see us to compare, it would be me in the fancy suite with him, not her."

"Do you really want a blind guy? He wouldn't appreciate your new boobs."

The blonde chuckled. "He's got hands, doesn't he? And really, who cares? He owns the hotel. He's filthy rich. I'd happily live my life off his dime while he stumbled around with his dog. I mean, who would be dumb enough to say no to that, even if he's blind?"

The waiter returned with Paige's drink and a fruit and cheese plate she didn't order. "What's this?" she asked.

"I got orders from Mr. Bishop to bring you a snack. He insisted that the baby needs to eat." He left the plate on a table beside her and put the pine-apple seltzer beside it. He didn't notice the gasp of the women nearby, but Paige did. If they thought she was pregnant with his child, their heads would probably explode. Let them think it.

"Thank you," she told the waiter.

"You've got to be kidding me," the blonde hissed. "God, I hope the baby looks like him."

That was all Paige could take. She cranked up her music and tried to focus on the snack Mano had sent for her. Even though she couldn't hear any more of their venomous words, she didn't need to. The damage was already done. What little ego Mano had built up in her over the last few days gave way, and she felt as ugly and unlovable as she had the day she found out Wyatt was with Piper.

She picked at the fruit and cheese because she knew she should, and eventually she tried to read. It was impossible to do with the music so loud in her ears, but she couldn't risk hearing any more of the women's conversation.

When she was done eating, Paige decided her time by the pool was over. She might as well go back upstairs to change and go shopping for a while. Maybe a little retail therapy would improve her mood.

Paige started gathering her things into her bag, finally removing her earbuds and noticing with relief that the women were now discussing their extensive grooming habits instead. As she stood up and slung her bag over her shoulder, she heard the brunette speak again.

"Aren't you going to get in the pool?"

"No," the blonde said. "I just had my hair colored before we came. My stylist said if I get chlorine on it, it will turn green. I don't like getting in pools, anyway. How do I know some kid hasn't peed in it?"

Paige tried not to roll her eyes as she left. Their chairs were nearer to the pool's edge than hers, so she had to get close to the water to move past them. Then she paused as she realized that she was leaving and she still hadn't gotten into the pool. Putting her bag down on another chair, she eyed the distance and slipped out of her shoes. She took a running leap, cannonballing into the pool right in front of the two women.

As she broke the surface, she could hear the women screaming about getting wet. A quick glance confirmed that the blonde was now completely soaked, including her hair. She really hoped that it did turn green.

Paige calmly climbed out of the pool and wrapped herself in a towel. As she left, she turned and gave a little wave to the women.

Damn, she thought as she disappeared down the path. That felt *good*.

"Let's go for a walk on the beach," Mano suggested. "The sun is about to go down."

Paige snuggled closer to Mano as they sat on the couch. "I'm happy right here."

"Perhaps, but in a few days, you can sit on the couch and do nothing whenever you want. You won't be able to walk along Waikiki beach and watch the sky change colors as the sun sets."

"Yes," she countered, "but I won't be able to do either of those things with you."

Mano hugged her tighter and placed a kiss on the crown of her head. "If your only requirement is being with me, I say you be with me while we walk on the beach."

Paige groaned but reluctantly sat up. Mano whistled for Hōkū, and they prepared to go downstairs. He hoped she didn't notice him slip the gift he bought her into the pocket of his cargo shorts. As he expected, she hadn't taken advantage of his offer to buy her something, so he'd taken the initiative to choose a gift for her himself. He was certain that he'd selected something far nicer and more expensive than she ever would've chosen on her own.

They headed downstairs and through the garden courtyard to the beach, where they slipped off their shoes. Hand in hand, they walked together along the shore. Mano could feel the warmth of the sun move lower as it sank into the sea. The water washed over their feet as they walked, Hōkū's paws happily splashing ahead of them.

"You were right," Paige admitted after a few peaceful minutes of walking. "This is better than the couch."

"I told you it would be. I bet you it will get even better, too."

Paige didn't question him, and after they got a certain distance from the hotel, Mano decided it was time to give her the gift. She'd been a little quieter and more reserved than usual today. He hoped that the gift would bring out the excitement in Paige that he was missing. "I want you to close your eyes," he said.

Paige giggled. "Don't you think at least one of us should be able to see where we're going?"

"We're not going any farther. Just hold still and close your eyes. If you don't close them, I'll cover them with my hand."

"Okay, okay."

Mano brushed his fingertips across her cheeks and felt her thick lashes resting there. "All right." Hōkū came to a stop beside them and Mano held Paige's shoulders steady. "Okay, keep them closed."

"I am," she insisted.

Mano reached down into his pocket for the large velvet box he'd gotten from the high-end jewelry store in the hotel. As quietly as he could, he opened it and removed the necklace from inside. He felt the clasp, opening it the way the jeweler had taught him, and then draped it around her neck. "Keep them closed," he insisted as he fastened the necklace.

"This is killing me," Paige said.

"I know. Okay, open your eyes."

Mano held his breath waiting for her reaction. As far as he could tell, there was none. No squealing, no jumping up and down. He was certain the jeweler in his own hotel wouldn't sell him something subpar. Six figures should at least get him a thank-you, if not an enthusiastic kiss.

"Did you open them?" he asked.

"Yes." Her answer was barely a whisper.

"And? Do you like it?" He hoped she would. The jeweler had helped him pick out an exquisite three-strand multicolor black South Sea pearl necklace. She'd told him the pearls alternated in size and shade from near black to a silver gray and were separated with ten carats' worth of small micro pave diamond pearls. The jeweler said the luster on the pearls was remarkable. He knew it was the ideal gift for her—a tiny piece of sand transformed into a beautiful, rare gem. It was the perfect memento of her time here, where he hoped that she, too, saw herself as a precious gemstone instead of a tiny bit of sand.

"I do," she said after a moment of hesitation.

Mano frowned. "You don't sound like you do. I thought you'd like it. I told you to pick out something and you didn't, so I chose this for you. I wanted to get you something nice to help you remember this week."

Paige put her hands on each side of his face. "I don't need an expensive necklace to remember this week, Mano. I'm certain I'll never forget it."

He was glad to hear that, but it didn't change anything. "Well, then consider it a thank-you gift. You've gotten me out of the hotel, forced me out of my comfort zone and helped me realize that maybe I don't need to spend every moment of my day at the resort."

"A simple thank-you would've been enough. This necklace is…"

She was resistant, and he was certain she had no idea how much it cost. "No, a simple thank-you is not enough. I bought you this necklace because I wanted you to have it, Paige. I can make up a million excuses you can shoot down, but that's the long and short of it. What good is all my money if I can't spend it on the things I want to spend it on? Please humor me and just accept it."

He heard Paige sigh heavily. "Okay. Thank you. It's beautiful, Mano." She leaned in and gave him a soft thank-you kiss.

When they parted again, they turned toward the hotel and started their leisurely stroll back. "How would you like to spend tonight, Paige? The Moonlight Luau is going on at the hotel if you'd like to see that. We could go out to eat somewhere where we could dress up and you can show off your new jewelry."

"I don't think I have anything to wear that would do this necklace justice. At the moment, I feel silly wearing it because I'm in denim shorts and a tank top."

"A beautiful woman wearing beautiful jewelry doesn't need a fancy dress."

"There's an idea," Paige said leaning in close to him. "How about we stay in tonight, order room service and I'll wear the necklace. *Just* the necklace."

Mano felt his whole body stiffen at her suggestion. His blood started humming through his veins, making him eager to return to the hotel. No matter how many times he had Paige, he wanted more. "A tempting offer."

He tried not to wish for his vision very often. It was the kind of hopeless yearning that succeeded only in fairy tales. Rapunzel's tears wouldn't cure him because this was real life. And yet, Paige painted a picture in his mind that he wished he could see for real.

Paige made him wish for a lot of things that he hadn't ever expected. She was so many different things in one person, and he'd never imagined he'd find a woman like that. He'd indulged in a handful of affairs over the years, but he'd always been happy to let them come to an end when their time together was up. He'd never been tempted to search one of them out, invite them back for another visit to the island or really even give them much thought once they were gone. They had fun together, but that was all.

Mano had the feeling that it would not be the same with Paige. This week was not enough. Their time together was not enough. Her melodic laughter and tender caresses would haunt him for weeks.

But was it fair to ask more of her? Mano didn't think so. Would another week be enough to soothe his soul? What if it wasn't? What if he wanted more? Longer? What if he was thinking about forever?

Mano choked down that thought and wished it away. Those sorts of fantasies were even worse

than hoping to see again. Why did he long so badly
for Paige? Why did it have to be the one woman
whose life was so complicated that their future together didn't really stand a chance? She had a life
in California, one that wouldn't be so simple to just
walk away from. She was certain the baby's father
wouldn't want to be involved in her life, but what
if she was wrong? Paige couldn't just take the baby
out of state, much less half an ocean away.

Lost in his thoughts, Mano stumbled as he
stepped into a hole in the sand. He landed face first
in the water, soaking his clothes and covering the
front of him in wet sand.

Hōkū whimpered beside him, licking at his ear
to make sure he was okay.

"Oh, my goodness!" Paige exclaimed.

She crouched down beside him and offered him
her arm to get up, but he wouldn't take it. He pushed
himself up on his own and wiped away the sand
from his face and chest. His jaw tightened with irritation. It had been a long time since he'd fallen.
He wished that it hadn't happened in front of Paige.

"Are you okay?" she asked.

"I'm fine," he said stiffly. He grabbed Hōkū's collar and took her hand, continuing down the beach.
Anger and irritation coursed through his veins as
they walked together. This was part of the reason he
didn't leave the resort. It was a carefully controlled
environment that left few hazards for him. Out in

the world, anything could happen. Hōkū couldn't see and avoid every obstacle in life.

It was hardly a major accident, but he knew the moment for what it was: a reminder. This entire line of thought about Paige moving to Hawaii to be with him was ridiculous. Even if Paige *would* stay, even if she loved him, even if the baby's father wanted no part in her life...he was still blind. He managed fairly well by himself, but would he be any help to her with the baby? More likely he would be an additional burden she didn't need.

"Are you sure you're okay?" Paige asked as they stepped off the beach and across the walking path to the Mau Loa.

"I'm fine," he insisted. They washed their feet off and slipped their shoes back on. "I've only bruised my pride."

Thankfully, Paige didn't press him about it again. They didn't even speak as they made their way through the grounds to the resort tower elevator.

"I've been thinking," Mano said at last. The words slipped out before he could really think it through.

"About what?"

Mano considered emptying his head into her lap. Maybe he was wrong and she could give him some insight or hope that they could have a chance together. Or perhaps not. She could shoot down the whole idea and the short time they had left together would be overshadowed by the dark clouds of her rejection. He needed to let the whole idea of a future go.

"About you wearing that necklace and not a stitch else." He covered with a sly smile.

"You're a naughty boy," she said with a laugh, clinging to his arm.

Better than a fool, he decided, as they headed back upstairs.

# Nine

Paige didn't feel comfortable wearing this necklace in public. Not because it wasn't beautiful or because she wasn't proud to wear it, but because she was afraid of getting mugged. She'd seen this necklace in the window of the resort jewelry store when she was walking around after the pool incident. Smaller, far less impressive necklaces had dropped her jaw with the price, so she couldn't even begin to imagine what he'd paid for this.

When she got home, she'd have to look into things like insurance and a safety deposit box. This wasn't the kind of thing you tucked away in your underwear drawer with your class ring and the tiny diamond earrings your parents bought you for graduation.

Once they were safely back in his hotel suite, however, Mano went to take a shower and she could finally let herself enjoy it. She sought out her reflection in the sliding glass doors and admired the necklace. It was amazingly beautiful with different shades of gray and sparking stones that would be cubic zirconia on anything she bought herself, but she doubted that was the case here.

"Paige?" Mano asked after exiting the bathroom sand-free a few minutes later.

"I'm at the balcony doors admiring my new pretty," she said.

Mano made his way over to where she was standing. He pressed his bare chest against her back and wrapped his arms around her waist. The palms of his hands rested protectively across her newly rounding belly.

She watched their reflection in the glass as he planted a kiss on her bare shoulder. It was a little surreal to watch herself in the door with a man like Mano holding her. No matter how he flattered her or how many times he worshipped her body in bed, she couldn't believe how she'd ended up right here, right now. She was supposed to be spending a week reading a paperback on the beach.

Mano was an unexpected and very welcome surprise in her life. They'd only been together for a week, and yet, it felt like so much longer. It seemed like he'd always been a part of her life. She honestly didn't know what she was going to do when that was no longer the case. They'd agreed to a no-strings fling—a vacation romance to keep her mind off reality for a while. That didn't include a future. And yet she couldn't stop herself from wishing for it.

Unfortunately, what she wanted didn't exist. Mano had offered to take care of her. As nice as that might sound on paper, there was no way she could accept it. She couldn't be around him, accept his money, raise her child, but not have him really in her life. If she moved to Hawaii, it was because Mano loved her and wanted her here with him. After their discussion in North Shore about Jenna and his emotional unavailability with women, she knew she was doomed. She'd made a joke out of it in the moment, but inside she'd realized that she was falling for a man who would never fall for her.

Mano's hands ran over her bare arms, his kisses sending a shiver through her body that made her skin break into goose bumps. Paige leaned back against him as he wrapped his arms around her and held her tight.

"I'm not ready to let you go yet," he said, echoing her own thoughts.

She only wished he truly meant it, in more than just the physical sense. All she could do was make the most of the time they had left together. "You don't have to," Paige said and turned in his arms to face him. "You can hold me all night if you want to."

She pulled her tank top up and over her head, revealing her bare breasts beneath it. She tossed her top aside so they could stand skin to skin. He was so hot to the touch. Paige was always cold despite the temperate climate of Southern California. Being wrapped in Mano's heat was like coming home to a warm blanket.

He kissed her then. It was the softest, most tender kiss they'd ever shared. There was no hesitation or resistance, no desire-fueled desperation, just a sweetness that made her eyes start to tear up. She was glad he couldn't see it. She didn't want to ruin this moment because her emotions were getting the best of her.

Maybe it was the pregnancy hormones. Yes, that must be it.

Paige took his hand and led him into the bedroom. She tugged away the towel from around his hips and then sat him down on the edge of the mattress. Her denim shorts followed the towel. Then, as they'd discussed, she was finally wearing nothing but the necklace.

The idea that he fantasized about her like this made her feel bolder. She stood between his thighs and took his hands in hers. She moved them all around her bare skin, then brushed his fingertips along the pearls at her throat. "As you requested," she said.

Mano's jaw clenched and he took a deep breath. Easing back farther on the bed, he took her hand and pulled her with him. Her body covered his as they lay on the bed together. Every inch of her molded against his hard muscles. He cupped her face and brought her lips to his again.

"What do you want me to do?" she whispered against his lips.

"Whatever you want to do."

Paige bit her lip, considering her freedom. She drew her legs up to sit astride him. It wasn't really a position she'd ever been comfortable in, but this was her chance to really, truly let go without feeling self-conscious.

Mano reached for one of their last condoms and slipped it on. She didn't need to wait for him. Paige had been ready the moment he touched her. His hands cupped her hips as she eased up and lowered herself onto him. The position pressed him deeper than ever before, filling her to where she was almost hesitant to continue. She slowed and let her body relax into it, finally seating herself fully against his hips.

Mano groaned and pressed his fingertips deep into her flesh. "Oh, Paige," he managed between clenched teeth. "You feel so good."

She did feel good. Her confidence increased with

his reaction urging her on. She planted her palms on the hard wall of his chest and slowly rocked forward. Thrusting him deep inside her, she curled her lips into a sly smile. She liked this. A lot.

Paige watched every flicker of emotion on Mano's face as she moved, studying what got the best reaction out of him. When he was on the brink, she backed away, coaxing him closer and closer to the edge. She, too, grew nearer her climax with every move she made. Their bodies seemed perfectly fit for one another, with no move possible that didn't feel amazing.

She'd never been this in control, this confident in the bedroom. It was a rush of excitement that urged her on. She wanted to know exactly how to move to make Mano crazy, how to touch him to make his jaw tighten and body tense.

But most importantly, she didn't want this moment to end. There was a finality about their coupling this time. It wasn't likely to be their last sexual encounter before she returned to the mainland, but the sands of the hourglass were slipping away. Tomorrow would be about her grandfather and saying goodbye. Then her life would pick up where she'd left it off. A life without Mano.

The tears returned to her eyes. Paige couldn't help it. Even as she moved slowly and tortured him, she felt the emotions start to overwhelm her. How had he become such an integral part of her life in such a short time? How was she ever going to make it without the man she loved?

Paige hesitated for only a moment when she realized where her thoughts had turned. There was no point in denying it. She was in love with Mano. She'd broken the rules of their fling and fallen head over heels for a man she could never, ever keep. There was no joy in the realization; her heart didn't overflow with elation and adoration the way she'd imagined it would when she finally fell for someone.

It was just as she'd told Mano that night after their first kiss. She couldn't get involved because her life was complicated. Now she'd gone and made it ten times more complicated than ever before.

Mano reached for her, pulling her back into the moment. "Kiss me, *pulelehua*," he said.

She leaned down and gave herself over to his kiss. Paige surrendered everything she had because she didn't know what else to do. She didn't know what the next year would bring, but she had this moment with Mano, and she would treasure every second of it.

As their lips joined together, his fingers pressed into her hips and moved her harder against him. The friction created a delicious tension inside Paige that she knew she couldn't resist for long. Within seconds, they both found their release and their voices mingled and echoed in the open air of his bedroom suite.

She collapsed onto the bed beside him, and he curled her body against his. "What am I going to do without you?" he whispered into her ear.

"Life goes on," she replied, knowing that for him it would. For Paige, living her life without him would be much harder.

"Why does the time go by so quickly in Hawaii?"

Mano turned to Paige with a frown. "What are you talking about?"

They'd been sitting on the balcony of his suite together while they drank juice and Paige watched the sunrise. It was hard to believe this was the last Hawaiian sunrise she would see. It seemed like only yesterday that she was standing alone on the beach at sunrise, wondering how she was going to spend all this time in Hawaii by herself.

"A week anywhere else would've taken far longer. It feels like I've only just arrived and yet I go home today."

He smiled and sought out her hand. "Have you considered that's because you've spent a good part of your trip in my bed? Time flies when you're having fun and all."

"Is that the problem?" she asked with a laugh. "It's all your fault, then."

Mano just shrugged off her accusations. "I told you I was a terrible tour guide." His expression grew more serious. "It is hard to believe that you leave tonight. What time is your grandfather's service at Pearl Harbor?"

"Two in the afternoon. Then it's time to pack up and head to the airport this evening."

"This is our last day together, then."

The words seemed to hang in the air between them. She didn't want to let go of this moment here with him. And yet she knew she had to. She'd cherished every moment of their last night together, especially when she'd fallen asleep cradled in his arms. Waking up had been bittersweet. Tomorrow would be back to reality. Back to home and plans for the baby. Back to her shift at the VA. Back to tell Wyatt he was going to be a father.

It had become too easy to lose herself here. She'd gotten used to room service and amazingly high thread count sheets. Her shower at home wasn't filled with coconut soaps and fluffy, freshly laundered towels. Her grandfather had given her this moment of paradise, but soon it would be time to face the life she'd ignored for the past week. She wished she could put off that eventuality for a little while longer, but she knew it would just hurt more if she did.

"I wish you could stay longer."

Paige sat up, startled, and pulled her hand away from his. He'd spoken the words that were on her mind, but she didn't dare say them aloud. He couldn't possibly mean what he'd just said. At least, not the way she wanted him to mean it. He probably wanted her to stay another week, not the lifetime she hoped for. "Don't say that," she chastised. "It will only make it harder for me to go home and deal with reality. Staying in Hawaii isn't an option, and you and I both know it."

"I don't know it. Who made that rule, anyway?"

"The universe did, Mano. And even if I *could* stay, what would it mean for us? Not much. You yourself said that you don't do relationships that last longer than a week."

Mano sat forward in his chair and rested his elbows on his knees. "You're the first woman I've met that makes me want to break that rule."

His words of longing for her made her chest ache, but she knew she couldn't let her feelings for him overtake her like they had last night. They'd urge her to make a hasty decision that she'd regret later, and in the end it would only complicate the matter further. "You say that now," she insisted. "I guarantee you'll be relieved when I'm gone."

Mano flinched as though she'd hit him. His brow furrowed deeply as he turned to her. "Why would you say something like that?"

Paige knew that she had to convince him of the truth. He would forget about her, and she'd rather he remember her fondly for a short while than grow tired of her and wish her away. "Because I know it's true. As much as I might like to be, I know I'm not the woman for you, Mano. We've come together for a short, beautiful moment in time, but it won't last. It can't. I'm sure there's someone here on Oahu that's perfect for you. Someone whose life isn't quite as complicated as mine."

"How do you know who's perfect for me?" There was an irritated edge to his voice.

"I know what I look like and you don't. I know you can do better. I want to thank you for everything you've said to me this week. It's really worked wonders for my self-esteem, but the truth is that you're out of my league."

"I am not," he snapped.

"Mano, if you really knew how I looked, you never would've laid a hand on me." That was the truth and she knew it. Those women by the pool had reminded her of the unavoidable reality of it.

Mano shook his head as he sat back in his chair and turned away from her. "That's not true. I know exactly what you look like."

Paige regarded Mano with suspicion. "Please tell me how such a thing is possible."

"Well, for one thing, I've touched you. Every inch of you. There's nothing boyish about you, Paige."

"It's not the same."

"Perhaps. But I also have a staff of a thousand here at the hotel. They are my eyes and ears. I asked around about you those first few days. They told me *exactly* what you looked like."

Paige's mouth dropped open. Could he really have known this whole time? It couldn't be true if he was sitting here, asking her to stay longer to be with him. And yet, she knew how often he wore that earpiece, how frequently he was in communication with his staff. It seemed perfectly natural, since they acted as his eyes around the hotel, that they would report on her to him if he'd asked.

"You think I've been operating under some kind of delusion this whole time, but I haven't. I know exactly what you look like, outside and in. Even a blind man can see the pure light that shines from inside you. You're a good person. I have spent this week with you, I've made love to you, because I like you just as you are, Paige."

She tried not to cry at his words. Never in her life had a man said that to her. All his assurances that she was attractive, all the compliments this week… she'd taken it all with a grain of salt because she didn't believe he knew the truth about her. Could he really have meant it all? He sounded so sincere.

"Do you want to know what a lot of my staff told me about you?" he asked.

Not really, but she supposed he would tell her, anyway. "What?"

"It really frustrated me at first because several of them didn't notice you at all. They would see me talking to you but couldn't tell me a thing about you. It seemed as though you were almost a ghost, invisible to everyone around you but me. I couldn't understand why so many of them didn't take notice of you. You certainly commanded my attention from the first moment we met."

"I ran into you. I'm sure those other people would remember me if I did that."

"That's the best way to get me to notice you, of course. But I couldn't help but wonder if you were deliberately wanting to be invisible and I was the only one you couldn't hide from."

"I don't deliberately try to hide," Paige began, but stopped herself. That was a lie and she knew it. "Okay, maybe I do. I've heard so many cruel and hateful comments over the years that maybe I've just wished myself out of existence and forgotten all about it. I've become accustomed to people not seeing me now. And really, I'd prefer that people didn't see me if all they have to offer are rude critiques. I'd rather be invisible than bullied."

Mano was quiet for a moment, turning back to the dark ocean as he seemed to be considering his words. "Paige, do you think that telling me all this is going to change my mind about wanting you to stay? It sounds to me like you're trying to convince me to let you go."

She sighed. In a way the exact opposite was true. She wanted to stay, to give in to the feelings she was holding back and throw away her whole life to remain here with him. But Paige had already made one major relationship mistake this year. She couldn't afford another. What would she have if she gave in to this and he changed his mind? Mano's whole adult life had been spent avoiding real intimacy. Did she really believe she was the woman who could change him for good? No. She didn't.

"I'm just beating you to the punch, darling."

Mano shook his head, his lips turned down in a disapproving frown. "You're ridiculous."

"Maybe, but I know how the fairy tales end for girls like me." She sighed. "Do you want to know what happened with the baby's father?"

Mano stiffened in his seat, but then he nodded. "Please."

"Okay, I'll tell you. He left me for my prettier sister," Paige said, spitting out the most painful part up front so the rest would be easier to tell.

"Ever since junior high when boys started looking at girls with thoughts of things other than cooties, Piper was the one they wanted. Through high school, college and beyond, the men have always preferred Piper, and for good reason. We're only a year apart in age and people always had a hard time believing we were sisters because we looked so different. She's the opposite of me in every way, with all the best parts of our parents. I've always felt like I got the leftovers."

"Describe her to me," Mano demanded. "I want

to know what it is about her that you think is so special compared to you."

"Well, for a start, her hair has natural golden highlights and a slight wave that makes it flow beautifully down her back. Mine is dull and stick straight, refusing to hold a curl for more than a few minutes. She's curvy in all the right places while I'm rail thin and built like a twelve-year-old boy. Her face is like an angel with big hazel eyes and full lips. My lips are thin and my nose and chin are too pointy. We just couldn't be more different."

"It sounds like it. But why would you compare yourself to your sister like that? If I compared my-self to Kal, I'd make myself crazy."

"Because," Paige argued, "that's what everyone does. My whole life I've been looked over for Piper."

"I don't understand it. You haven't described any of the important things," Mano noted. "You'll have to forgive me, being blind and all, but my priorities are a little different. Is she smart or caring like you? Is she funny and kind? Would she spend her days caring for injured veterans or would she rather get her nails done?"

Paige was startled silent. She wasn't quite sure how to respond to that question, even though the answer was quite evident to her. Piper wasn't vapid and thoughtless, she just had different priorities. She was a hairstylist, so her focus in life was entirely visual. But she wasn't selfish. She'd tried to give Paige multiple makeovers, but they rarely took.

"You're in the minority, Mano. Most men can't help themselves around her, and as I mentioned earlier, Wyatt was no different. When Wyatt left me for Piper, it was just the latest incident in the story of my life. It was like I didn't exist to him any longer. He didn't even have the nerve to tell me we weren't dating anymore. He just ghosted me—stopped calling and texting—and then he showed up at a family event with my sister on his arm."

"Wyatt is obviously an ass, but what kind of sister would do that? Is she that cruel?"

Paige shrugged. "No, it's more a matter of ignorance. Piper is oblivious to everyone but herself. She always has been. I think to her it was natural for a man to prefer her over me, so I shouldn't be so hurt about it."

"Hurt about it?" Mano nearly shouted. "She steals the father of your child, but you're not allowed to be hurt about it?"

"Neither of them know I'm pregnant. I haven't told anyone but you."

"So that's why the baby's father won't be in its life? He'll be too busy being its uncle instead?"

That sounded terrible. A part of her hoped they would break up before that became a reality. "Something like that. Even if they stopped seeing one another, it's not like I'd take him back. I know better.

I've had better, thanks to you. But I know what we have isn't something that can last. Tomorrow I'm getting on a plane to go home. I'll go back to reality and will finally have to deal with everything I've pushed aside while I was here.

"While I'm decorating a nursery and reorganizing my whole life, you'll be here, running your hotel. It may take a few weeks, or even a few months, but you'll forget about me. You'll spend another week with another woman, and life will go on. Maybe someday I'll cross your mind and you'll wonder how I am and if the baby turned out to be a boy or a girl. But that's all the future the two of us have together, Mano. It was just a fling. A wonderful one, but a fling."

# Ten

"I'm going to get in the shower," Mano said.

After breakfast at sunrise and their depressing conversation, Mano had been at a loss of what to say to Paige. There was no convincing her to stay, no convincing her that she was good enough for him. She didn't want to drag him into the complicated life she was living, and the finality of her words convinced him that was the end of the conversation.

They'd returned to bed for a nap and a leisurely round of goodbye sex. Mano had taken his time making love to her, knowing it was the last time. Now that it was over, he knew he had to get up and walk away from it all before he did something stupid.

Crawling from the bed, he disappeared into the

bathroom to get ready for the service. His thoughts were scattered as he shampooed his hair and considered his options.

Paige was distracted and distant today, which wasn't unusual considering they were about to sink her grandfather's ashes into the ocean. It felt like more than that, though. It was like she was anticipating the end and pulling away from him before it was over. That was probably the smart thing to do. How much longer did he have? Not much. Hours.

She'd insisted that she couldn't stay and that he wasn't serious about the two of them, but he knew that he was. This didn't feel like any other time before. Paige was different. He felt different. He just had to find a way to convince her of it. She wasn't like the other women in his life, and he wished she could understand that. He wanted her to stay. He wanted to help her raise that baby. Their baby. One day, he hoped that he could love her so well and so completely that she could even forget about Wyatt and what he'd done to her.

A plan formed in his mind as he stepped out of the shower. He would tell her how he felt. He would say the words he'd never said aloud before. That would convince her he was serious and then she would stay. Wouldn't she? He wrapped a towel around his waist and filled the sink with warm water to shave. Mano was rinsing the blade one last time when a strange sound in the bedroom caught his attention. It took Mano a moment to realize it might be Paige's cell phone. No one had called her the whole week, so he hadn't heard it ring yet.

"Hello?" he heard her answer.

He wasn't trying to listen in on her conversation, but he found it difficult not to with only a door between them.

"Wyatt? Why are you calling me?"

Wyatt? Just the mention of the man's name made Mano's blood start to boil in his veins. He turned off the water to hear them better.

"Piper will be furious if she knows you're calling me…No, I'm not at home," she responded to him. Her voice sounded stressed. "I'm in Hawaii… Yes, Hawaii."

Mano was nearly holding his breath as he listened to half of their discussion. Paige had sworn up and down that she wouldn't take Wyatt back. She said she didn't really want him involved in her life, or the baby's life, but she'd do what was right and tell him about the child. Her extended silence meant he had quite a bit to say for a man who had vanished from her life without an explanation not long ago.

"You're right, Wyatt, we do need to talk but not right now…No, I'll be home tomorrow morning. You know I've got to bury Papa today."

Mano could only think of one reason why Wyatt was calling Paige. He wanted her back. Unless he'd left his laptop at her apartment or something, it was the only thing he could come up with.

"I know," Paige said. "It was extremely difficult for me. I just can't talk about it right now. Call me tomorrow afternoon, okay? All right. Goodbye."

Mano waited a moment, drained the sink and then stepped out of his bathroom with his towel still slung around his hips. "Did I just hear you talking to someone?" he asked casually.

"Uh, work called," she said, the lie evident in her voice even if he hadn't overheard the conversation. "They thought I would be back in time to work the day shift tomorrow, but I told them I wouldn't be in until Sunday. I don't think I can go straight from a red-eye flight to work a twelve-hour shift the next morning."

He nodded and turned back to his bathroom to finish getting ready. His mind was racing with thoughts as he dried his hair with a towel. Why had she just lied to him about who called? There was only one real answer that made sense—that she hadn't been entirely truthful with him about her feelings for Wyatt. He'd called her out of the blue wanting to see her. Why? Had Piper dumped him? Was he going to make a play to get Paige back?

And more distressing…would Paige actually take him back after everything he'd done?

The thought made Mano sick to his stomach. Paige deserved so much better than a man like

Wyatt. And yet, if he really did have a change of heart, who was Mano to interfere with that? He was the father of her child. Wouldn't it be best for everyone if they reconciled and raised their new family together?

The only odd man out of this scenario would be Mano, but he would survive. As Paige insisted, maybe he would forget about her in a few weeks or months and continue on as though she hadn't touched his heart. Or maybe he would throw himself into his work, heartbroken, and she'd never know it.

Either way, he knew it wouldn't really matter as long as she was happy. A future with her baby seemed to excite her; would having an active father in the baby's life be even better? It would certainly make things less complicated for her. She wouldn't have to uproot her whole life to be with him. Her child would have a father. His real father. It would tie everything up into a neat bow.

It would crush Mano. Make him that much more emotionally unavailable. But that was what he needed to do. If there was a chance in hell that Paige could reconcile with the baby's father, it would be selfish of him to go out there and declare his feelings for her and beg her to stay.

He wasn't thinking clearly, Mano realized. He was letting emotion cloud his decision-making skills. Paige was right. It was better if she went home. He would forget. He would move on. If he did manage to convince her to stay and then one day regret raising another man's child and uprooting her from her whole life, then what? It was better to let her life take the path she'd chosen, and that was to go home. If that meant going home to Wyatt, that was none of his damn business in the end.

With a sigh, Mano combed his hair and splashed his face with aftershave. He just needed to keep his mouth shut.

Paige clutched her grandfather's urn as the boat took them out to the USS *Arizona* Memorial on the far side of the harbor. It was temporarily closed to tourists, allowing Paige private access for the ceremony. She took in the markers that identified the locations of the various boats in the harbor and the real ships still in service to the far left.

The memorial was a gleaming white building that seemed to float above the water. Beneath it, she knew, were the sunken remains of the *Arizona* and the sailors who lost their lives that day so long ago. Only a few small parts of the ship were visible above the waterline.

A man in full dress blues took the urn from her as they stepped off the boat and onto the dock. Mano took her arm, escorting her up the ramp to the memorial with Hōkū just ahead of them. They followed a large procession that included the firing squad, the officer carrying the urn and a bugler.

Inside, the memorial was filled with navy officers and personnel dressed for the most formal of occasions. As Paige was the only family there for the ceremony, there was only one row of chairs set up. They were led there and seated in front of the massive memorial wall. From floor to ceiling, the names of all the men who died the day the USS *Arizona* was bombed by the Japanese were etched into marble.

In front of the monument were two large rectangles made from the same marble. On it were the names of the sailors who had returned to the Arizona to be interred, like her grandfather would be. The stone memorials were draped with purple and white orchid leis. The names were fewer, but just as impactful to Paige. Twenty, forty, sixty years later… these men never forgot that day or the brothers they lost. They all chose to return to be with them in the end. Including her grandfather. His name was the latest to be etched into the stone. She was certain he was one of the last survivors remaining.

Seeing all those names at once brought a tear to Paige's eye. She tried to hold it in. Not because she was embarrassed to cry—it was her grandfather's funeral, after all—but because once she started, she was pretty certain she wouldn't be able to stop.

She'd already cried her tears for Papa. She cried most of those while he was still alive and clinging to existence no matter how miserably his heart was failing him. No, today she was mourning something different.

The loss of love.

Paige could already feel it slipping away. She was the only one to blame for her situation, but it didn't make it any less painful. Could Mano not understand how hard it was for her to say no to him? It was agonizing. It broke her heart to do it. Of course she wanted to stay. She could easily come up with some extended fantasy about what their life could be like together if she just threw caution to the wind and never returned home.

But that wasn't reality. If nothing else, Paige prided herself on being practical. Nothing about that scenario was practical. Especially the part where she expected Mano to raise her child as his own.

She couldn't ask that of him. Even as much as she loved him. Maybe because of how much she loved him. Paige wanted him to have a family of his own. It would happen for him, she just knew it, if he would open up to the possibilities. It was that, more than his disability, that was holding him back. He didn't believe his happiness was possible, so it wasn't.

Paige supposed she was just as guilty of sabotaging herself. Because she thought she was unattractive, she assumed that was what people saw. It was a cycle that fed on itself. Mano had helped to disrupt that, convincing her to feel better about herself and what she had to offer. Perhaps if she felt that way on the inside, she would attract more positivity in her life.

Not love. Just positivity. She didn't have room in her future or her heart to love anyone but the baby. Paige knew that as hard as it had been to cope with what had happened with Wyatt, it would be nothing compared to losing Mano. She didn't love Wyatt the way she loved Mano. It would take a long time for her to heal and let someone else in.

She didn't know what that call today from Wyatt was about. He hadn't spoken two words to her since he'd run off with Piper. She got the feeling he was sniffing around for something. Had her sister broken up with him and he was looking to come back? Fat chance. She might be naive, but she wasn't stupid. Whatever he wanted from her was irrelevant, really. She would meet with him, tell him about the baby and ask what kind of arrangements he wanted to make. That was it. Even if he declared his love for her, she wouldn't bite. She knew what real love felt like now, and it wasn't what he was offering.

The ceremony started with the chaplain reading scripture. Her grandfather's urn was placed on a table draped with the American flag. Mano took her hand for support, but she could feel the strained energy radiating off him like a wave. He hadn't been the same since their discussion this morning. She had rejected him before he could reject her, so she supposed he had a right to feel unhappy about it. One day he would understand why she had to do it.

The admiral in charge of the base stepped up to speak. It was an amazing honor to have such a high-ranking officer at her grandfather's service, but it was such a rare and important occasion that many officers in the navy wanted to attend. He spoke about the bombing and the soldiers like her grandfather who survived. He thanked Paige for his service to the country and for his dedication to his fallen brothers.

Two uniformed navy men picked up her grandfather's urn from the table and carried it to the window of the memorial where it was handed over to a dive team. Paige watched as the diver secured the urn, then slipped beneath the oil-slicked waters to the belly of the ship. All the navy officers silently saluted as he was interred.

"Unto Almighty God," the chaplain continued, "we commend the soul of our brother departed, and we commit his body to the deep; in sure and certain hope of the resurrection unto eternal life, through our Lord, Jesus Christ, Amen."

He continued with the benediction. When that was finished, the firing squad fired three volleys and the bugler played "Taps." The loud noise was a startling contrast to the rest of the ceremony. The vibration of the shots threatened to shatter what was left of her nerves.

By the time the flag was folded and presented to her, Paige feared a breakdown was coming. They were escorted out of the memorial and took the boat back to the shore. There, they got back into the hotel town car that had brought them to the service.

The farther she got from Papa and his final resting place, the more alone she began to feel. He was the one who understood her. He encouraged her, supported her, when the rest of her family didn't understand their awkward youngest daughter. Without Papa and without Mano, who would she have now? It would be just her and the baby, together against the world. Would that be enough? She supposed it would have to be.

As the car returned to the highway toward Waikiki, Paige was unnerved by how quiet it was. Mano hadn't spoken since they'd left for the service. He was a good enough man to stand by her through the memorial, but she could feel him pulling further away by the minute. Part of her had known this moment would come, but now that it was happening, it hurt more than she expected. It was almost as though she could feel him physically ripping away from her, leaving a gaping hole in his absence. She thought that trying to take a step back sooner would ease the pain, but it didn't. It only made her wish she'd clung more tightly while she had the chance.

"Thank you for going with me today," she said

quietly. Paige clutched the flag in her arms and held it fiercely in lieu of the man she loved.

"You're welcome. It was my honor to join in on the ceremony to honor a sailor from such a historically important event." The words were stiff, almost practiced like a campaign speech.

"I can't imagine having to sit through that by myself. It was much easier having you there with me."

He didn't turn to look at her. With his dark glasses on, he simply stared ahead through the windshield. "No one should have to. I don't understand why the rest of your family didn't fly out here for this."

"My grandfather didn't want them to. He wanted a memorial ceremony in California for everyone to attend, but this service to be more private."

"Private is immediate family. This is beyond private. I have to say you have an odd family. At least compared to my own. If one of ours dies, you're not keeping the others away unless you rise up from the grave and drive them off."

"You're lucky."

Paige imagined that the upcoming months with her family would be difficult. Her parents wouldn't be thrilled about her unplanned pregnancy, especially when they realized their other daughter was dating the baby's father. While a landscaper might be as good as Paige could do, they'd certainly disapprove of Piper lowering her standards.

She didn't expect a big baby shower or a large showing of people to help her plan and prepare. Brandy would be there, of course. She had no doubt her friend would help her celebrate, but it wouldn't be like it would if she had a family like Mano's. The way he spoke about them, she imagined being smothered by their excitement over the baby. Would there be traditional Hawaiian music at their shower? Would they bury a whole pig wrapped in banana leaves in the backyard to roast over hot coals? Would his grandparents fawn over her rounded belly and bless the baby with a traditional Hawaiian name?

For the first time, she allowed herself to wish that Mano was the baby's father instead of Wyatt. That would make everything simpler. Then she wouldn't have to ask Mano to raise another man's child. She wouldn't feel guilty about staying on Oahu to be with him. There was also the fact that she loved Mano. Loving the baby's father was a critical element that she was missing from her reality. She didn't just not love Wyatt, she despised him. That wasn't the way it should be.

Although she'd vehemently rejected his suggestion that she stay, it was getting harder by the minute not to change her mind. She didn't like him turning a cold shoulder to her after how passionately he'd treated her all week. It was one thing to want to stay. It was another to know he felt the same way. If he would walk away like she meant nothing to him, it would still be hard, but she could leave knowing their affair was one-sided. She let her heart get involved, and that was her own fault.

And yet…

The car pulled up outside the hotel. Paige knew her chance to change her mind was slipping away. Would it change things if she told him how she felt? Would she just embarrass herself? Things were ending either way.

"Mano?" she said just before they got out of the car.

He paused and turned to her. "Yes?"

"I…" The words stuck in her throat. With his dark glasses covering the expression on his face, she couldn't read his emotions. She couldn't tell how he'd accept her words. He just seemed to radiate this protective wall that she wasn't sure she could penetrate.

"I've got a pretty busy schedule this afternoon," he said when she couldn't get the words out. "I've arranged for the car to take you to the airport whenever you're ready."

Paige felt her heart drop in her chest. "You're not seeing me off?"

He shook his head, his expression aggravatingly neutral. "I'm sorry, I can't. But I want to thank you for a lovely week. I enjoyed our time together very much. I hope you enjoyed your visit here at the Mau Loa, and I wish you the best for your future."

Without so much as a hug or a kiss goodbye, he opened the door and he and Hōkū got out of the car. He tipped the driver and disappeared into the hotel without the slightest hesitation.

Paige couldn't move. She couldn't breathe. Her heart started to crumble in her chest and she could feel every painful crack as it fell apart. The tears rushed down her face then. The seams holding her together unraveled completely, and she collapsed into broken, heaving sobs in the back of the car. It was an angry, ugly cry, making her face a blotchy red and her nose run. She simply couldn't hold it in anymore. Everything that had happened over the last month—her grandfather's death, the pregnancy, Wyatt's betrayal—had snowballed together with Mano's cold rejection.

She let herself give in to it. She didn't know if the driver was watching, but she really didn't care. Her life was unraveling before her eyes, and if she wanted to sit in the back of the car and cry, she damn well would.

When she was out of tears, she reached for a tissue she'd stuffed away in her purse for the funeral. Paige dabbed away the tears and blew her nose before throwing it away. This was what she thought she wanted, but she was wrong. So wrong. She pushed him away in self-defense and now she regretted it. She would rather confess her love to him and be rejected than to receive this cold, neutral goodbye. She'd hurt him. And now he'd hurt her. She had to fix this.

With a surge of bravery, she climbed from the town car and ran into the hotel after him. She glanced every which way around the lobby, but he was nowhere to be found. Paige dashed over to the concierge desk.

"Did you see which way Mr. Bishop went?" she asked.

The man looked at her suspiciously, then shook his head. "I'm sorry, I didn't."

"Please," she insisted. "I have to tell him something very important."

"I'm very sorry, Miss Edwards, but Mr. Bishop has requested he not be disturbed while he works in his office this evening."

"But I—"

"He most specifically noted that he not be disturbed by you, miss," the concierge interrupted. "I'm sorry. I hope you enjoyed your time here at the Mau Loa. If there's anything we can do for you today before you check out, please don't hesitate to ask."

The polite, practiced speech mimicked Mano's parting words and felt like a slap in the face. He didn't want to see her. The man seemed pretty firm on his stance. There was no amount of begging or pleading that would get her behind the desk and into the business area of the hotel where Mano was hiding away.

That left her with no choice. "Thank you," she said softly and turned away. Paige sought out the elevator to return to her room.

It was time to pack and say goodbye to Hawaii and Mano for good.

# Eleven

It was a long overnight flight home with a layover in LA. She should've slept or watched a movie to pass the time on the plane, but instead, she'd stewed in her thoughts.

Paige hated the way she and Mano left things. He'd seemed to completely shut down when she told him she couldn't stay. She wanted to. Her heart ached at the thought of telling him no, but how could she stay? He didn't really understand what he was taking on. He wasn't just getting her in the bargain, and it wasn't fair to burden Mano with another man's child.

Anyway, did he really think they had a future together? The man who didn't date anyone longer than a week? What if she said yes, quit her job, gave up her apartment and moved to Hawaii, only to have him change his mind? Then what would she do? It was bad enough that it would break her heart, but as much as she might love him, she couldn't do that to her child, either.

Exhausted, Paige finally arrived home early the next morning, slipped the key into her apartment door and stumbled inside. She dropped her bags on the floor, then shouted in surprise as she noticed a figure in her apartment, sitting on her couch.

Her heart was still racing double time when she realized it was her sister, Piper. "What the hell are you doing here?" she asked. She was too tired and emotionally spent to use her polite filter. Especially with the woman who had run off with the father of her child. Not that she wanted him any longer.

Piper stood up to greet her anxiously. Paige noticed her normally attractive face was blotchy and red and her eyes were puffy. She'd been crying. "I came by because I knew you were coming home today."

"What do you care?"

Piper flinched. "How was Papa's service?"

Paige folded her arms protectively over her midsection. "It was very nice. They took some professional pictures at the ceremony that they'll be sending to our parents. They should get them in a week or so."

Paige felt awkwardly trapped at her front door. She didn't want to get any closer to her sister. She wanted to collapse into her bed, but Piper was in the way. "You didn't bring him here with you, did you?" It was the kind of thoughtless thing her sister would do. She wasn't deliberately hurtful, she was just oblivious to other's feelings.

"No," she said with wide eyes. "Wyatt…is gone." Piper broke down into tears again, but Paige had a hard time feeling sympathy for her.

At the same time, she got the feeling that her sister wasn't leaving anytime soon. "I'm going to make some coffee," she said. She'd have to use up her daily allotment of caffeine to get through this.

As the coffee started brewing, she noticed her sister standing in the entryway to the kitchen. "So what happened? Did he leave you for someone prettier?"

Piper winced at her sister's cutting accusation. "I don't know. Maybe. We didn't really talk about it. I just came home from work one day and he was gone."

"You don't know why?" Paige asked, pouring them each a mug full of steaming brew.

"I have my suspicions. He kept asking me what Papa left me in the will. I finally told him yesterday that he didn't leave me anything. That Papa left almost everything to a wounded veteran charity. I don't think he expected that. I think he was sniffing around me…around both of us…in the hopes that we'd inherit a fortune when our grandfather died. When I came out of it with nothing, he took off."

That made sense to Paige. She'd met Wyatt when he was working for her grandfather. He had first-hand knowledge of the sprawling estate and how much money the ailing man had to be worth. Paige must've been a convenient target for him. "That's probably why he called me yesterday. Maybe he thought I got something in the will even if you didn't. I feel stupid," she said. "It sounds as though he would've left me no matter what. He just jumped ship earlier because he thought he could get the money and a prettier woman in the meantime."

She held out a mug to Piper, who accepted it. "I'm so sorry, Paige. I don't know what the hell I was thinking. He was just so…"

"Mesmerizing." Paige remembered that much.

"Yes. And charming. And handsome. When he spoke to me, I felt like the most important person in the world. I got wrapped up in it. I never should've let myself get anywhere near him when I knew you two were dating. I never meant to hurt you. I mean, you're my sister."

Paige didn't know what to say. Would her sister be here apologizing if she hadn't been dumped? She wasn't sure. Instead, she just shook her head. "It's okay. I'm over Wyatt." And she was. She was madly in love with another man who lived an ocean away.

"Are you sure?"

"Absolutely."

Paige turned to face her sister and noticed that Piper's gaze zoomed in on her just-rounding belly. She knew better than anyone that Paige had always been rail thin, even underweight. A sudden belly was more than just too much food on her recent vacation. Her eyes grew round and wide, then she looked up at Paige with her mouth agape.

"You're pregnant?"

Paige looked down and stroked the tiny belly she'd earned as she started her second trimester. "I guess this shirt is tighter than when I wore it last. I should've tried it on before I packed it." She sighed and nodded. "Yes, I'm pregnant."

"With Wyatt's baby?" Piper didn't need her sister to answer that. The crestfallen expression on her face was proof enough of that. "Oh my god, Paige!"

Paige set her coffee down just in time to receive the sudden embrace of her sister. Piper clung to her with new tears dampening Paige's shirt. She thought she'd cried all she possibly could in the car yesterday, but she'd been wrong. In her sister's arms, she found she couldn't hold them in. The tears rolled down her cheeks almost faster than her body could produce them.

They stood like that for several minutes until their emotions were spent and their eyes had dried. At last, Piper pulled back and wiped her cheeks.

"You come sit down right now," she said, launching into her older sister bossy self.

Paige was too tired to argue. She took a seat at her dining room table and Piper sat down beside her.

"How far along are you?" she asked.

"Almost fourteen weeks. I didn't find out about the baby until after…" Her voice trailed off, unable to finish with the words *after you stole him away*.

"Does he know?"

Paige shook her head. "I was going to tell him when I got back."

"Oh no," Piper said. "You're not likely to track him down. His phone is disconnected. His apartment is vacant. He's not even working for that landscaping company anymore. Wyatt seriously split town when he was done with us."

Paige felt a sense of relief when she heard the news. "To tell you the truth, I'm okay with that. I don't really want Wyatt in the baby's life. I just knew it was the right thing to do." She stared down at her coffee, thinking about all the decisions she'd made. "How could I let myself get in a position like this with a man like that?"

"He was a snake, Paige. He whispered whatever you wanted to hear into your ear and you melted like butter. I did the same thing. You're not to blame for this."

"It's not just Wyatt," Paige began before bursting into tears again. "It's Mano, too."

Piper perked up in her seat. "Mano? Who is Mano?"

"He's the man I'm in love with," Paige managed between sobs.

Piper put a hand on Paige's shoulder. "Tell me everything."

So she did. She'd never really been one to share with Piper, but she had to talk to someone. Paige started at the beginning and told her about everything that happened on her trip to Hawaii. How she'd been intrigued by Mano's attention, how he hadn't seemed to be able to get enough of her. How broken he seemed to be, but how much he'd improved even over the short time they were together. How she'd let herself fall in love with a man even though she knew it wouldn't work out because she was a fool.

"He asked you to stay? That's a pretty big deal."

Paige shrugged it away. "At best, he's infatuated with the idea of us. The reality would never work. How can I ask him to raise another man's child? I can't ask him to do that, especially knowing that this might not last."

"You're absolutely certain you won't change your mind?"

"Yes. He never wanted to be a burden on a woman, and I refuse to be a burden on him. I don't think he thought it through enough to understand what he was asking."

Piper looked saddened by the way their enchanted vacation romance had ended. Paige understood.

"He only proposed a week. That's all it was ever meant to be."

At last Piper got a more cheerful expression on her face that reminded Paige of their mother when she was getting fired up. "You know what? Everything is going to be fine. You're going to get through this, and you're going to have the most amazing baby ever. You're going to be a great mom and you'll be so much better off without some loser in your life. Okay?"

Paige nodded and sniffled away the last of her tears. Her sister was right. She had a baby and a future to focus on now. She needed to make the most of that.

"Quit moping, Mano. I don't know what your problem is, but it's Tūtū Ani's day. Act happy for her."

"Of course I'm happy for her," Mano said to his brother, although it sounded more like a growl. Kal might have a point, but he couldn't help it. He'd been like this since Paige left on Friday. He'd tried to take a step back, protect himself from the sucker punch he knew was coming, but it still hurt. He'd much rather be at the hotel moping privately and not bringing down the family birthday festivities, but he didn't really have a choice.

He'd opted to find a corner where he could sit with Hōkū and be out of the way. These things were always too chaotic for him to walk around much. Even his own family had the tendency to forget he was blind and trip him up, especially the children, who didn't really know better. From what he could hear, the women were fussing in the kitchen, the men were preparing to dig up the kalua pork from the pit in the backyard, and he was no good to any of them.

Mano heard the squeak of the metal chair beside him and knew Kal had sat down. "So what's with you?" he asked. "Even Hōkū looks depressed. The last time we talked, you seemed pretty psyched about your semiannual romance. Did it not end well? Did she get clingy or weird about it?"

"The opposite, actually. Things were going great. We were having an amazing time together. I was beginning to think I wanted more than just a week with Paige and I told her so. But she left, anyway."

"That's a lot to spring on a woman after a week together. I mean, how did you tell her? Did you ask if she could come back and visit? Confess your undying love and ask her to move here? Propose marriage after her grandfather's memorial service?"

Mano felt his jaw tighten at his brother's probing questions. He didn't really want to talk about this. It was too fresh. "I told her that I wasn't ready for it to end and asked if she'd consider Honolulu as a potential future residence."

"A potential future residence? Tell me you didn't say it like that."

"I don't remember what I said now. All I remember is that she said no."

"I can imagine she had a lot to think about. And you didn't exactly sweep her off her feet from the sounds of it. For a woman to pack up her whole life, give up her job and move here, she needs more than just the idea that you two might continue to date."

"I know." He'd run it through his mind a million times. But a part of him was too scared to push it any further. "I didn't know what else to say, so I just let her go."

"I thought that's how you liked it. Easy and string free."

Mano shifted Hōkū's harness back and forth in his hands. "It is how I liked it. Until I met her. Paige changed everything…but it's complicated."

"How complicated can it be?" Kal asked. "You either have feelings for her or you don't. Do you?"

Mano swallowed hard. "Yes."

"Are you in love with her?"

He hadn't been certain then, but since Paige left, he'd been miserable. Heartsick. It felt just like when Jenna left. Only worse because then he was a child losing a sweetheart and now he was a grown man losing the woman he loved. "Yes."

He could hear Kal sigh and shift in his seat. "Man. This woman really got to you. I didn't think I'd see the day. Tell me what's so complicated about it. It sounds pretty straightforward to me."

This was the part of the story, Mano knew, that would change everything. "Paige is three months pregnant with another man's child."

"What?" Kal nearly shouted, then leaned in closer and whispered it again. He'd likely drawn looks from the family.

"You heard me. It's not as simple as I love her and we can start a life and everything is hunky-dory. There's things she has to deal with back at home, like the baby's father. He called her the other day and wanted to talk. I can't get in the way of her reconciling with the baby's father. And even if they didn't, she can't just move to Hawaii if he wants any kind of visitation. She also would be moving over two thousand miles away from her family and any support system she might need to raise her baby."

"That's true. But what you don't know is if she loves you. If she does, none of those other things matter. You didn't tell her. For all she knew this was just a promise of another week-long fling, not a lifetime commitment. And a pregnant woman in her position isn't messing around. If she does love you, she doesn't just want another week of romance. She wants your love in return and she wants you to love her baby as your own."

That was the other issue he wasn't quite sure how to address. Paige had been so adamant about not staying, he hadn't really thought their future through. Was he ready for fatherhood? In one week, he'd gone from being a confirmed bachelor to a man in love. Could he make the leap to family man and raise Paige's baby as his own child?

"Could you do that? Raise another man's child?" Mano asked his brother.

Kal sat thoughtfully for a minute. "It is just the same as dating a single mother with older children. If I loved the mother, I'd love the child. I don't think it would be hard since you would be there through most of the pregnancy. You'd be there when she delivered, and you'd get to hold the child in your arms. That's powerful stuff. I think in that moment, it doesn't really matter who the biological father is anymore. And besides, you're blind."

Mano winced, following his brother's logic until the end. "What does that have to do with anything?"

"Well, I would think it would be easier for you to ignore that it isn't your biological child. If the kid is born with red hair and freckles, that's a physical reminder that you wouldn't have to deal with. If you and Paige had children together, there wouldn't be anything to physically distinguish the child that is yours from the child that isn't, at least not to you. This is one instance in which being blind is perfect."

"Being blind is never perfect," Mano grumbled.

"You know what I mean, Mano. If you love this woman and you want to be with her, you have to tell her."

Mano hadn't expected this kind of guidance from his brother. Kal was as stubborn a bachelor as he was, although his reasoning was different. To hear his brother encourage him to throw caution to the wind and chase after Paige and her baby was a revelation.

"Do you really think I could? What would she say? What if she says no?"

"You absolutely could. I don't know Paige, and I can't guess how she feels about you, but it sounds like something serious happened this week. She might be scared of taking the leap the same way you are. Making a big gesture could make all the difference."

"But if it doesn't?" Mano pressed.

"If it doesn't, then you did all you could. You come home content in knowing that you aren't the first man to fall in love with a woman that didn't love you back. Then you move forward with your life. Simple as that."

It didn't seem simple. None of it was simple. He hadn't left the islands since before his accident. Getting on a plane with Hōkū, traveling to San Diego, tracking down Paige and confessing his love was anything but simple.

"Why would she want to love me, Kal? Even if I

love her and her baby, she's still inheriting a broken man. I'm never going to have my sight back. Does she want to raise a family with a man that can't contribute one hundred percent?"

"You know what?" Kal snapped. "You're full of it."

"Excuse me?"

"You heard me. You've been blind for over a decade. You run the Mau Loa like a corporate shark. You charm the ladies, you take care of yourself and Hōkū. Yeah, things would be easier if you could see, but you've learned how to live your life without your vision. You'll learn how to be a lover, a husband and a father without your vision, too. You just have to want to do it. You're only a burden on yourself because you allow it."

A roar of voices came from Mano's right. He turned his head to listen and was pretty certain the pig was up and ready. There was a commotion to follow as food was taken out to the long tables on the lawn.

"It's time to eat," Kal said.

"I know." His hand gripped Hōkū's lead. Part of him wanted to act on Kal's suggestions before he could change his mind. He could walk out the door right now and get a cab to the airport. He could be in San Diego tonight.

Then he heard his family start to sing to his grandmother. He took a deep breath and steeled his resolve. Kal was right. He would go to Paige, but he wouldn't rush things. He'd enjoy the day with his grandmother, make his plans and ensure that when he touched Paige again, he'd never ever have to let her go.

Mano stood and followed Hōkū to join the others in his grandmother's celebration. Before he could fall into line to make a plate, one of his aunts came up to him.

"Mano," Aunt Kini began, "Tūtū Ani would like you to sit with her to eat since she hardly gets to see you. Why don't you go ahead and I'll make you a plate?"

This was the aunt who treated him like he was helpless. "I can make my own plate, Aunt Kini," he tried to argue.

"I know that, Mano," she chided and put a hand on his cheek. "You run a whole empire. You can make a plate for yourself. But why? Today you don't have to conquer the world on your own. Your family is here. Let me do this for you and enjoy a few moments with your grandmother."

Mano couldn't argue with that. At least this way he wouldn't have to ask what each thing was in front of him and try to balance a plate in one hand while holding on to Hōkū with the other. He still needed to learn that accepting help wasn't the same as accepting defeat.

"Thank you, Aunt Kini."

"She's over to your left about ten paces," she said before disappearing into the crowd of his family.

Mano turned and started in the direction she provided, stopping when Hōkū sat down. "Tūtū Ani?" he asked.

"I'm here, child."

He felt his grandmother's hand grasp his. She guided him to a chair beside her at the table. *"Hau'oli Lā Hānau, Tūtū."*

*"Mahalo*, Mano. Are you enjoying the party?"

Mano shrugged. "This is your party to enjoy, not mine."

Ani made a thoughtful sound with her tongue, then laid her hand on his knee. "Who is she, *mo'opuna*?"

He perked up in his chair. How could she know there was a woman on his mind? He hadn't mentioned Paige to anyone but Kal. "What do you mean?"

"Mano, you think just because you are blind everyone else is, too. You look absolutely heartsick. What has happened? Why didn't you bring your lady today?"

"Because she went home Friday."

"But you love her. Why did you let her go?"

Mano stiffened in his chair. Even with his sunglasses on, his grandmother saw everything. He realized then that the problem was his feelings went far deeper than he'd imagined. "I don't know, Tūtū."

"You should go to her. Tell her how you feel. Then give her this."

Ani took his hand and placed something cold and metallic in his palm. "What is it?" he asked.

"It's my peridot engagement ring. The stone is native to the big island and has been in our family for generations. Your grandfather was given the ring by his mother. And now I'm giving it to you."

Mano didn't know what to say. He knew exactly which ring she was talking about. She'd worn it every day he could remember. The stone was a brilliant green octagon set in platinum with tiny diamonds around the edge. It was art deco in style, and almost a hundred years old. He couldn't imagine his grandmother would ever part with such a precious piece of jewelry. "But Tūtū, this is your ring."

"No, this is a family heirloom, no more mine than anyone else's. Give it to your love. Bring her back to Hawaii and begin your life together here. I insist."

"I would love to, but it's not that simple."

"What about love is simple, Mano?"

She was right. Kal was right. He needed to take their advice and act before Paige disappeared from his life forever.

"Why are you still sitting here, *mo'opuna*?" Ani asked.

"It's your birthday party," he insisted.

"Hopefully it will not be my last. You can make it up to me by attending the next one with your new bride. Go!"

Mano raised his grandmother's hand to his lips and kissed it. "Thank you, Tūtū," he said before getting up and making his way out of the house. He slipped the ring into his coat pocket and called the hotel to send a car for him. He was a short drive and a long plane flight away from Paige, and he wasn't going to waste another second.

# Twelve

Paige stood with her hands planted firmly on her hips. "Absolutely not," she said to her stubborn patient, Rick. "If you want a pudding cup, you need to walk with me down the corridor to get it."

"Are you a nurse or a sadist?" Rick snapped bitterly.

"A little bit of both. You've been fitted with that new prosthetic for a week now, and the doctor says you're to walk on it at every opportunity. The more you use it, the less it will hurt. You can even use the walker or the crutches," she offered.

"I'm not taking orders from a woman in scrubs with kittens on them."

Paige looked down at her purple scrubs and the

cartoon cats wearing tutus on it. She had to wear scrubs every day, so she tried to keep it lively with fun designs. "They're not just kittens, they're ballerina kittens. They're tough cats, and they're not interested in your excuses, either. If you want the pudding, you're coming with me."

Rick glared at her from his hospital bed. She knew it hurt to use his prosthetic, but he had to get past that or he'd never regain an active lifestyle again. She hated being like this, but sometimes with soldiers you had to antagonize them like a drill sergeant to get results.

"It's twenty feet, Rick. Just past the nurses' station. You can totally do it."

Rick finally flung his sheets back and sat up, placing both feet on the ground. "Give me the damn walker," he said, and she scooted it over to him. He pushed himself up, and with a wince they started down the hallway together.

"You're doing great," she said in a bright voice as they neared the snack station. "Chocolate or vanilla?" she asked.

"For this, it better be chocolate. With a Percocet chaser."

Paige smiled. "You got it." She got the pudding and spoon and started walking with Rick back to his room.

"Have you seen him?" she heard one of the nurses ask Brandy.

"No. Who?"

"He's the most beautiful man I've ever seen in real life. It's a shame he's blind and can't see how handsome he is."

Paige usually tried to ignore most of the other nurses she worked with. Today, however, their words caught her attention. She tried to focus on Rick, getting him the last few steps back to his room.

"How do you know he's blind?" Brandy asked.

"The sunglasses and the service dog. They don't let just anyone into a hospital with a dog, you know."

Paige's heart stuttered in her chest and she froze in place.

It couldn't be. It just couldn't be. Paige refused to let herself believe that it was Mano. That was ridiculous. He didn't want to leave the resort; the idea of him flying to San Diego was out of the question. Besides…why would he come chasing after her? He was the one who had used his employee as a bouncer to keep her away from him.

"Is something wrong?" Rick asked.

Paige's eyes widened as she realized she'd stalled her patient on his walk. "I'm sorry. Just a few more steps." She tried to focus on helping him into bed and getting him settled. That was more important. The minute she rushed out of the room she'd be disappointed, anyway. It was a veteran's hospital;

there were bound to be blind men with service dogs here who weren't the one she was desperate to see.

She tugged the sheets up and swung the bedside table over Rick's lap. She placed two pudding cups and a spoon on it for him.

"Two?"

"You earned it. I'll be back with that Percocet in a few."

Rick immediately dove into a pudding cup, freeing Paige to return to the nurses' station. She made a note in his file and tried to ignore her gossiping coworkers.

"It's a big hospital. I doubt he's coming up here," Brandy said. "Where was he?"

"In the gift shop. I ran down for a candy bar on my break a minute ago. He was getting flowers."

No. Paige shook her head and logged the dose of pain medication she was about to take to her patient.

"Excuse me," a man said from behind her. "Do you know where I can find Paige Edwards?"

She knew the voice in an instant, but she was certain her mind was playing tricks on her. She shot up and turned in his direction.

It was Mano. He was there in one of his tailored suits with his Wayfarers on. His hair was slicked back and his face clean-shaven. He was clutching a bouquet of crimson roses in his hands. She almost wanted to reach out and touch him to make certain this wasn't a hallucination. Mano wasn't just off the resort property—he was on the mainland. Thousands of miles from his comfort zone. Why?

"Paige?" one of the other nurses said. There was a noticeable incredulity in her voice.

"Brandy, would you please give this to Mr. Jones for me?" She handed the cup with two pills to her and walked around to the outside of the nurses' station.

When she got closer, she heard the telltale thump of Hōkū's tail on the wall. Mano immediately turned in her direction. "Paige?"

He was here. He was really here. "Yes?"

"I'm so relieved to find you," he said with a smile. "This has been quite the adventure for me so far."

"Congratulations on getting out and about," she said cautiously. "I'd tell you to check out the zoo, but all you'd get out of it is the smell of elephant dung."

Mano didn't laugh. He was far too focused on her. He took a few steps forward, closing the gap she'd deliberately left between them. "I didn't come here for the zoo." He reached out and handed her the bouquet of flowers. "These are for you. I hope they're as pretty as I imagined they are."

Her heart started pounding so loudly in her chest she was certain he would hear it. She accepted the bundle of bright red roses. "They're lovely, thank you. I'm confused, though. Why are you here, Mano?"

"I wanted to tell you that I'm a fool."

"A text would've sufficed," she said coolly.

"No, it wouldn't. I had to come here in person so you would understand how serious I am about this. I never should've let you walk away from me."

"It wasn't really your choice," she argued, and yet she knew that she would've turned and ran into his arms if he'd only asked her to. Hell, she'd tried and was cruelly shut down.

"Not entirely. You made your decision then and you can make your decision now, but I can't help but think the outcome would've been different if I hadn't been too scared to say what needed to be said to make you stay."

Mano didn't look like the kind of man who was scared of anything, much less of something as simple as words. Didn't he know he could tell her anything? "And now?" she asked. She bit anxiously at her lip as she awaited his response.

He reached forward and sought out her arm. His warm palm glided along her skin to her wrist and wrapped her hand in his own. "I'm still scared. Waking up with you gone was like waking up in the hospital all over again. I'd lost everything and it's terrifying. But I've got to say it, anyway. I came all this way because you need to know that I love you."

There was a loud gasp. Paige thought it might have come from her, but when she turned to the nurses' station, she realized both her coworkers were watching them like a soap opera on television.

"Let's go down the hallway and finish this in private," she said. Paige didn't really want them in her business. If this ended poorly, the whole third floor would know about it before the shift was over. She loved Brandy, but she was a blabbermouth.

"I don't want to do this in private. I want everyone to know how I feel about you," Mano insisted. "I want to rent a billboard and shout it from the rooftops. I'm not going to push my feelings down anymore because I worry about getting hurt. I realized it hurt more to lose you knowing I didn't try my damnedest to keep you with me than to spill my guts and have you walk away, anyway. At least then, I would've tried."

"Mano…" She didn't know what to say. Her thoughts were racing as his words spun around in her brain. He loved her. Did he really, truly feel that way? She almost couldn't let herself believe it.

"Don't," he said, squeezing her hand. "I know that tone of voice. You're about to tell me all the reasons why we can't be together. The distance and the baby and anything else you can come up with. I don't care about all that. You may see them as obstacles, but to me they're just challenges that can be overcome. All I know is that I love you more than I've ever loved a woman in my entire life. A week was not long enough. A year isn't long enough. I want you in my life for always. You and the baby."

Paige's mouth fell open. She couldn't believe what he was telling her. The baby had been the one issue she was certain they wouldn't be able to get past.

"I know that Wyatt called you the other day. He probably wants you back and he's a fool not to. I told myself I should step back and let the two of you have another chance, but I just can't. I love you too much, Paige."

He thought she and Wyatt were reconciling? She never should've lied to him about the call. She hadn't wanted Mano to know she spoke to him, not because they were anywhere near a reunion, but because she was embarrassed that she answered the phone when she saw his name.

She stepped close to him and reached up to pull off his sunglasses. She wanted to see his face—his whole face—when he said this to her. Then, and only then, could she look in his eyes and see if he was telling the truth. "Say it again," she whispered.

Looking down at her, Mano clutched her hand against his chest. She could feel his heart pounding in his rib cage nearly as fast as her own.

"I love you, Paige Edwards. I love everything about you, and that means I love that baby, too. It's a part of you, half of you, and that means it's going to be an amazing child. And if I have anything to say about it, it's going to be my child."

His child? "I don't understand. How could it possibly be—"

"If we are married when the baby is born and

my name goes on the birth certificate, he or she will legally be mine. I'll fight anyone who would say otherwise."

Paige stiffened. Any minute now she was going to wake up. This was like some extended fantasy playing out in her mind. She'd been awake too long and slept too little the night before. Any second now, she would snap out of it and realize that she'd fallen asleep in the break room over a lukewarm frozen meal.

Mano let go of her hand and reached into his lapel pocket. There, he pulled out a small wooden box. He opened the lid and presented the ring to her for her approval. It had a glittering green stone the size of her thumbnail in the same bright color as the foliage around the Mau Loa. It was surrounded by baguette diamonds and set in either white gold or platinum, she didn't know or care which.

Mano removed the ring from the box and held it up to her. "This ring has been in my family for generations. The peridot was mined on the big island over a hundred years ago. My grandmother gave it to me this weekend. For you. She insisted that no other ring would do if I wanted you to be my bride. And I do, more than anything. So Paige, will you do me the honor of being my wife?"

The silence seemed to go on for an eternity. All Mano could do was stand there, holding the ring

like a dolt, and wait for her to answer. He couldn't
see her reaction. All he knew was that she hadn't
run away this time.

"Paige?" He palmed the ring and reached out
to touch her face. Her cheeks were wet with tears.
"You're crying. Why are you crying?" he asked.
"I'm sorry. Do you not like the ring? I can get you
a different one. Tūtū won't mind."

"Don't apologize. And you are absolutely not
getting me a different ring. That's the most beautiful and special ring you ever could've chosen. It
would be an insult to Tūtū and your whole family
if I turned it down for some boring old diamond."

The panic started to subside in him. Despite her
tears she sounded...happy. "So you *do* like it?"

"I do."

"Then will you please say yes and save me from
all this suspense?"

"Mano, I want to say yes."

The anxiety returned. Why was it that Paige
could never just go with her heart? She always had
to rationalize and analyze everything. "Do you love
me, *pulelehua*?"

"I do. You know that I do."

Okay, one obstacle down, he thought with a sigh
of relief. "Did you like Oahu? Would you be happy
living with me in Honolulu?"

"Oahu was amazing. I would be happy living

with you there, but I don't know that I want to raise a family in the hotel. I want my child—"

"Our child," he insisted.

"*Our* child to have a normal life, and that means a house and dinners that are cooked, not delivered on a silver platter by room service."

That was a concern he could easily address. He would give her anything she wanted if she would just say yes. "Absolutely. That's how I grew up, and you're right, that's how it should be. We visited the hotel a lot, but we didn't live there. We had a home. And if that's what you want, we'll go house hunting the second we return. You can have whatever you want, Paige. You only have to ask it of me."

"Then what about my work? You know how important it is to me. I want to continue working with veterans, even if it's only on a part-time or volunteer basis while the baby is small."

Mano had anticipated this one. "There is an amazing VA hospital in Honolulu. I'm certain they would be lucky to have you there for an hour or forty hours a week."

He waited for Paige's next argument, but there was a long silence instead. Was it possible that he'd actually gotten through all of their excuses not to be happy?

"Mano," she said at last, this time in her smallest voice. "Are you sure this is what you want? You've gone your whole life dedicated to being a no-strings-attached bachelor. If I say yes, and I accept your ring and move to Oahu, I can't have you changing your mind."

"You keep trying to talk me out of what I've already decided. Why do you keep giving me an out from this, Paige?"

"Because usually the person takes it." The emotion in her voice made his heart ache in his chest. He wanted to go back in time through her life and punch all the people who had made her feel like she didn't deserve this.

"I love you, Mano. I do. But my heart can't take it if you offer me this fantasy and then snatch it away. You really, truly want me as I am, with this baby as your own? Wyatt has vanished, so I'm doing this by myself."

"No, you're not. You're not doing anything alone again. I'm going to be at your side until you're sick of me. And once the rest of my family finds out about you and this baby…you'll wish for peace and quiet. I'm not going to change my mind, Paige. I wouldn't dream of doing that to you, to me, or to our child. We're going to be a family. Or we will be, if you would just say you're going to marry me."

"Okay." Paige moved closer to him, pressing her body against his. "I will marry you." Her hand caressed his cheek, and then her lips met his.

He felt a rush of happiness and relief wash over him as she kissed him, her acceptance of his proposal still ringing in his ears. She was going to marry him. He hadn't ruined this.

Then an odd sound captured his attention. Mano reluctantly pulled away from Paige, turning his ear toward what sounded like…applause. "What is that?" he asked.

Paige giggled softly in his arms. "Those are my patients and the rest of the nursing staff," she said. "Apparently, your dashing proposal has drawn a crowd of them from their rooms."

Mano laughed. He hadn't expected that. "Well, then let's put this ring on your finger and make it official."

He held out the ring and slid it up Paige's finger until it nestled tightly. This was met with another round of cheers and an enthusiastic bark from Hōkū.

He hugged her tight against him. "So, can we get out of here?" he asked. He didn't want to wait any longer than he had to to bed his new fiancée.

"I have two hours left on my shift."

Mano frowned. It was just like his Paige to be so responsible. She'd probably insist on giving two weeks' notice, as well. Any fantasies about sweeping her into his arms and flying her on a private jet back to Hawaii within the hour were likely just that.

"Did you really just say that?" a woman asked.

Paige shifted in his arms. "Brandy, I can't just walk out and leave you guys."

The woman snorted. "You're too nice a person,

Paige. If a hunk proposed to me and wanted to kidnap me and take me to Hawaii, I wouldn't even say goodbye. I'll explain to the supervisor what happened, although she'll hardly believe me. Now go on, get out of here."

Brandy was joined by the shouts of what sounded like a dozen soldiers surrounding them and encouraging Paige to run off with him. Mano was glad to have backup on this.

"Come on, Paige," he said. "What do you say we play hooky today? You work too much and you need to get out more."

"My own words coming back to haunt me," Paige said.

"You and I are going to play hooky together for the next fifty years. We're going to teach our daughter to paddleboard and deep-sea fish. We're going to—"

"Wait," Paige interrupted. "What makes you think this is a girl?"

"I had a dream about her the night you left, like my grandparents did about me."

"And what did you see?"

"I saw you running down the beach chasing after a little girl with long brown hair. She was tan from the sun and leaping through the waves like she was born to be there."

"So we're having a girl?"

"Yes, *'Eleu.* It means energetic and agile."

Paige giggled, the melodic laughter reminding him of the first day they met. The day that changed his life forever. "It sounds like I'm going to have my hands full."

Mano smiled and gave her a kiss. "I can't wait."

\* \* \* \* \*

*If you loved this story of pregnancy and passion*
*from Andrea Laurence,*
*don't miss the sequel*
*THE BABY PROPOSAL*
*available December 2016!*

*And be sure to pick up these other books from*
*Andrea Laurence!*

*WHAT LIES BENEATH*
*MORE THAN HE EXPECTED*
*BACK IN HER HUSBAND'S BED*
*HIS LOVER'S LITTLE SECRET*

*Available now from Harlequin Desire!*

*\*\*\**

*If you're on Twitter, tell us what you think*
*of Harlequin Desire! #harlequindesire*

# COMING NEXT MONTH FROM

## HARLEQUIN® *Desire*

### Available November 8, 2016

#### #2479 HOLD ME, COWBOY
*Copper Ridge* • by Maisey Yates
Rich-as-sin cowboy Sam McCormack wants nothing to do with ice princess
Madison West, but when they're snowed in together at a mountain retreat,
their red-hot attraction quickly burns through all their misconceptions...

#### #2480 ONE HEIR...OR TWO?
*Billionaires and Babies* • by Yvonne Lindsay
As promised, Kayla became the surrogate mother for her late sister's
baby—and she's expecting again! But when complications arise, the only
person who can help is the sexy billionaire donor who doesn't yet know
he's a dad...

#### #2481 HIS SECRETARY'S LITTLE SECRET
*The Lourdes Brothers of Key Largo* • by Catherine Mann
Organizing Easton Lourdes's workaholic life is a full-time job, and
secretary Portia Soto is the best at keeping things professional. But
when a hurricane sends her into her boss's arms—and his bed—the
consequences will change everything...

#### #2482 HOLIDAY BABY SCANDAL
*Mafia Moguls* • by Jules Bennett
Dangerous Ryker Barrett owes the O'Shea family everything—and he
proves his loyalty by keeping his hands off Laney O'Shea. Until he not only
seduces her, but gets her pregnant, too! Will his dark past keep him from
forever with her?

#### #2483 HIS PREGNANT CHRISTMAS BRIDE
*The Billionaires of Black Castle* • by Olivia Gates
Ivan left the woman he loved once, to protect them both. But when
he saves her from an attack, he can no longer stay away. Will keeping
Anastasia as his bride mean overcoming the sinister events that shaped
him?

#### #2484 BACK IN THE ENEMY'S BED
*Dynasties: The Newports* • by Michelle Celmer
Roman betrayed Grace years ago. So when the wealthy ex-soldier
swaggers back into her life, she's prepared to turn the tables on him. But
she can't resist the unexpected desire between them—even as his secrets
threaten to tear them apart...

---

HDCNMI016

# REQUEST YOUR FREE BOOKS!
## 2 FREE NOVELS PLUS 2 FREE GIFTS!

**HARLEQUIN®**

*Desire*

ALWAYS POWERFUL, PASSIONATE AND PROVOCATIVE

**YES!** Please send me 2 FREE Harlequin® Desire novels and my 2 FREE gifts (gifts are worth about $10). After receiving them, if I don't wish to receive any more books, I can return the shipping statement marked "cancel." If I don't cancel, I will receive 6 brand-new novels every month and be billed just $4.55 per book in the U.S. or $5.24 per book in Canada. That's a savings of at least 13% off the cover price! It's quite a bargain! Shipping and handling is just 50¢ per book in the U.S. and 75¢ per book in Canada.* I understand that accepting the 2 free books and gifts places me under no obligation to buy anything. I can always return a shipment and cancel at any time. Even if I never buy another book, the two free books and gifts are mine to keep forever.

225/326 HDN GH2P

Name                                      (PLEASE PRINT)

Address                                                                    Apt. #

City                              State/Prov.                          Zip/Postal Code

Signature (if under 18, a parent or guardian must sign)

Mail to the **Reader Service:**

**IN U.S.A.:** P.O. Box 1867, Buffalo, NY 14240-1867
**IN CANADA:** P.O. Box 609, Fort Erie, Ontario L2A 5X3

**Want to try two free books from another line?**
**Call 1-800-873-8635 or visit www.ReaderService.com.**

* Terms and prices subject to change without notice. Prices do not include applicable taxes. Sales tax applicable in N.Y. Canadian residents will be charged applicable taxes. Offer not valid in Quebec. This offer is limited to one order per household. Not valid for current subscribers to Harlequin Desire books. All orders subject to credit approval. Credit or debit balances in a customer's account(s) may be offset by any other outstanding balance owed by or to the customer. Please allow 4 to 6 weeks for delivery. Offer available while quantities last.

**Your Privacy**—The Reader Service is committed to protecting your privacy. Our Privacy Policy is available online at www.ReaderService.com or upon request from the Reader Service.

We make a portion of our mailing list available to reputable third parties that offer products we believe may interest you. If you prefer that we not exchange your name with third parties, or if you wish to clarify or modify your communication preferences, please visit us at www.ReaderService.com/consumerschoice or write to us at Reader Service Preference Service, P.O. Box 9062, Buffalo, NY 14240-9062. Include your complete name and address.

HDI5

*Rich-as-sin cowboy Sam McCormack wants nothing
to do with ice princess Madison West, but when
they're snowed in together at a mountain retreat,
their red-hot attraction quickly burns through all their
misconceptions…*

*Read on for a sneak peek of
HOLD ME, COWBOY
the latest in Maisey Yates's New York Times bestselling
COPPER RIDGE series!*

"Are you going to suggest that I need *you*?" she asked,
her voice choked.

Lightning streaked through his blood, and in that
moment, he was lost. It didn't matter that he thought
she was insufferable, a prissy little princess who didn't
appreciate anything she had. It didn't matter that he was
up here to work.

All that mattered was he hadn't touched a woman in a
long time, and Madison West was so close all he would
have to do was shift his weight slightly and he'd be able
to take her into his arms.

"Well," he said, "you have a couple of the essential
ingredients to have yourself a pretty fun evening. All you
seem to be missing is a good man. I'm not very nice,
Madison," he said, leaning in, "but I could damn sure
show you a good time."

She should throw him out. She looked over at him, and her libido made a dash to the foreground. That was the problem. He irritated her. He was exactly the kind of man she didn't like. He was cocky; he was rough and crude. However, there was something about the way he looked in a tight T-shirt that made a mockery of all that very certain hatred.

"Are you going to take off your coat and stay awhile?" That question, asked in a faintly mocking tone, sent a dart of tension straight down between her thighs.

She could *not* take off her coat. Because she was wearing nothing more than a little scrap of red lace underneath it. And now it was all she could think of. "It's cold," she snapped. "Maybe if you went to work getting the electricity back on rather than standing here making terrible double entendres I would be able to take off my coat."

The maddening man raised his eyebrows, shooting her a look that clearly said Suit yourself, then set about looking for the fuse box. She let out an exasperated sigh and followed his path, stopping when she saw him leaning against the wall, a little metal door between the logs open as he examined the switches inside.

"It's not a fuse. That means there's something else going on." He slammed the door shut and turned back to look at her. "You should come over to my cabin."

*Don't miss*
*HOLD ME, COWBOY*
*by* New York Times *bestselling author Maisey Yates,*
*available November 2016 wherever*
*Harlequin® Desire books and ebooks are sold.*

www.Harlequin.com

# Whatever You're Into... Passionate Reads

Looking for more passionate reads from Harlequin®?
Fear not! Harlequin® Presents, Harlequin® Desire and
Harlequin® Blaze offer you irresistible romance stories
featuring powerful heroes.

### ✦HARLEQUIN® *Presents*

Do you want alpha males, decadent glamour and jet-set
lifestyles? Step into the sensational, sophisticated world of
Harlequin® Presents, where sinfully tempting heroes ignite a
fierce and wickedly irresistible passion!

### ✦HARLEQUIN® *Desire*

Harlequin® Desire novels are powerful, passionate and
provocative contemporary romances set against a backdrop of
wealth, privilege and sweeping family saga. Alpha heroes with
a soft side meet strong-willed but vulnerable heroines amid a
dramatic world of divided loyalties, high-stakes conflict and
intense emotion.

### ✦HARLEQUIN® *Blaze*

Harlequin® Blaze stories sizzle with strong heroines and
irresistible heroes playing the game of modern love and lust.
They're fun, sexy and always steamy.

Be sure to check out our full selection of books
within each series every month!